"*Pino!*" she
and giddy.

'*Va bene, cara Luc...* ....
saying, assuring her that she was safe as she clung
to him.

There was an almost irresistible temptation in the
deep, accented voice and in his warm breath on
her face. Her mouth was ready for the touch of
his lips—soft at first, then harder and fiercer.
There was a recklessness in his kiss, but Lucy
sensed a helpless rage beneath his abandoned
behaviour, something almost approaching despair.

And then she thought of the lovely Gabriella.

Margaret Holt trained as a nurse and midwife in Surrey, and has practised midwifery for thirty-five years. She moved to Manchester when she married, and has two graduate daughters. Now widowed, she enjoys writing, reading, gardening and supporting her church. Margaret believes strongly in smooth and close co-operation between obstetrician and the midwife for safe care of mothers and their babies.

Recent titles by the same author:

REMEDY FOR PRIDE
AN INDISPENSABLE WOMAN

DOCTOR ACROSS THE LAGOON

BY
MARGARET HOLT

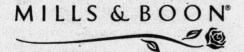

MILLS & BOON®

To Mary, Maureen, Frances and all my writing friends who
have helped and shared.

*First published in Great Britain 1997
Harlequin Mills & Boon Limited,
Eton House, 18-24 Paradise Road, Richmond, Surrey TW9 1SR*

© Margaret Holt 1997

ISBN 0 263 80052 0

*Set in Times 11 on 12 pt. by
Rowland Phototypesetting Limited
Bury St Edmunds, Suffolk*

03-9703-44644-D

*Printed and bound in Great Britain
by Mackays of Chatham PLC, Chatham*

CHAPTER ONE

LUCY was trying very hard to give her full attention to the present speaker, but it was not easy with that pair of bold black eyes appraising her from the other side of the Sala di Congresso.

She was well used to admiring glances from men, but this was hardly the time or the place—the time being the second afternoon of the Venice Convention on Cardiovascular Disorders, and the place being the Ospedale Civile, well known as a centre for the subject under review.

Seated beside her MP father and flanked by his private secretary and Meg Elstone, the shorthand typist, Lucy had *felt* those inquisitive eyes upon her before she turned her head to confront their owner, a complete stranger. Her mother would have called it ogling and not to be encouraged and, of course, Lucy would not dream of doing so.

Only when she *did* just happen to glance his way there he still was, raising his jet-black eyebrows and nodding to her in a way that plainly showed his approval of what he saw. Drat the man! Lucy felt that she should be offended at such uncalled-for attentions from a—who *was* he? Some junior official, perhaps, or maybe one of the interpreters? A journalist, probably, with no sense of what was proper behaviour at such an important conference as this.

Except that the man was quite wickedly attractive,

that is, if you happened to care for those typical Latin features, all flashing dark eyes and wide, sensual mouth—and Lucy was not at all sure that she did. She would definitely not look in his direction again.

She fixed her large, violet-blue eyes on the speaker, now at last concluding his dissertation on Occupational Occurrence of Arteriosclerosis. She was not able to concentrate very well because of his monotonously droning voice, as well as the distraction of those dark glances which she resolved to ignore totally from now on. Just pretend that he wasn't there. . .

Yet there he *was*, actually giving her a little wave with his fingers. Really, he was impossible!

The speaker finished and, in the conversational buzz which followed, Aubrey Portwood leaned over and spoke quietly to Lucy in his usual unobtrusive way.

'Excuse me, Lucinda—the next speaker is Findlay d'Arc, the obstetrician and gynaecologist. You said you particularly wanted to hear his paper on Cardiac Conditions in Pregnancy.'

'Oh, yes, of course! Thank you, Aubrey.' She had not forgotten but gave the private secretary a polite smile of acknowledgement for his reminder, while at the same time giving her father an affectionate poke in the ribs. He opened his eyes, having dozed off, and sat up quickly.

'Has that chap finished at last, darling? He must have sent half the delegates to sleep!'

'Shh, Daddy!' hissed Lucy, glancing quickly around. 'I've heard that the next speaker's very good.'

'Really?' Sir Peter Hallcross-Spriggs beamed at his daughter, and spoke to the typist.

'Get your notepad ready, Meg, and take down the most important points, will you?'

'Oh, *no*, Daddy, don't bother poor Meg with yet another transcription,' protested Lucy, who had heard the shorthand typist's resigned sigh. 'I can take all the notes I need, honestly.'

She gave a little giggle, and several heads turned to look at the young woman accompanying Sir Peter. With her masses of dark brown hair, framing a classic oval face, Lucy appeared to be a typical English beauty, the product of a privileged upbringing and education at a top girls' school. Few observers were likely to discern the hidden heartbreak, the haunting self-doubt beneath her coolly attractive exterior as she held her pencil and pad in readiness for the next presentation.

When she casually turned her eyes in the direction of the tiresome stranger she found, to her surprise, that he had vanished. Where on earth could he have gone, she wondered—the men's room? And would he return to his place in time to hear the next speaker? Lucy felt quite put out at his sudden disappearance.

The chairman of the convention was making an announcement.

'Unfortunately Mr d'Arc is unable to be present this afternoon, and Dr Giuseppe Ponti has kindly agreed to read his paper for us.'

Dr Ponti was introduced as a general practitioner of Venice, based on the Lido. A tall figure ascended the podium, and adjusted the microphone to his height.

Lucy gasped. He was none other than the man who had been so rudely annoying her for the last half-hour! Briefly nodding to the assembly, he began to speak and almost immediately he commanded the undivided attention of all present. With his strikingly dark eyes and a quirkily humorous twist to his mouth, his varying expressions brought a series of case histories vividly to life.

There was a vitality about him which Lucy found impossible to ignore. He would suddenly turn to a particular section of the lecture hall to make a point, holding his hand out to them, palm uppermost, as if demanding a response; or he would hold up a long forefinger to emphasise a warning.

His voice had a wide range of pitch, and if his accented English occasionally mispronounced words there was no mistaking the sense which they conveyed. He was totally riveting, and when the reading was finished a spontaneous burst of applause arose from the whole hall.

'By Jove, Lucinda, if they could all put it over like that, I'd get a lot more out of it,' observed Sir Peter. 'Though I'm sure you'll do just as well when you give our paper on Thursday, darling.'

Lucy certainly intended to try.

Scarcely had the applause died down when Ponti began again, this time reading in Italian—which Lucy could follow fairly well, having studied the language for A levels. With the freedom and fluency of his mother tongue, Ponti's interpretation of another man's work made the same compelling listening— even to non-Italian speakers, having just heard the English version.

He conveyed the dilemma of being faced with a woman with valvular heart disease, manageable in normal circumstances but deteriorating as the additional strain of pregnancy took its toll.

'You now have another life to consider, a second patient whose welfare is as important to the woman as her own,' he told them sombrely, and went on to outline the choices to be made, the decisions to be shelved until after the delivery of the child and the mode of that delivery. All these problems were set before the conference with a poignant immediacy; the delegates saw this woman before them, a real mother expecting a real baby.

Lucy herself was not exempt from Ponti's spell and found the sensation oddly disquieting, for she experienced a chill of dissatisfaction with her life and career.

What career? asked a cynical voice in her head, bleakly persistent in spite of all her efforts to dispel it; in vain did she tell herself that her present job in medical statistics was the right outlet for her particular talents, allowing her time to fulfil the social engagements expected of the Honourable Dr Lucinda Hallcross-Spriggs.

Suddenly her heart gave a jolt as she saw Ponti looking straight at her across the hall. The sonorous Italian phrases that rolled from his lips spoke of the electrocardiographic changes that might be seen in the maternity patient with mitral stenosis. What should be done with her? he asked his audience.

'*Che cosa fa adesso?*' he demanded. What do you do now?

To Lucy the words were a direct personal

challenge, almost an accusation, and she dropped her
eyes before his searching look. Of course she was
being ridiculous, she told herself, for how could he
possibly know her history?

She was somewhat half-hearted in her applause at
the end.

'I say, jolly good!' exclaimed her father, clapping
vigorously. 'What d'you say to asking that young
fellow to give an Italian version of *our* paper,
darling?'

Lucy shrugged. 'Quite honestly, I don't think it
would be appropriate with such a different kind of
subject, Daddy—all those figures and percentages,'
she said doubtfully.

Ponti smiled his acknowledgement of the enthusiastic reception and held up his arms in a double wave
to the delegates.

Aubrey Portwood bent his silvering head close to
Lucy's ear and whispered, 'Rather like an actor
taking a curtain-call, don't you think, Lucinda?'

He laughed shortly, and Lucy tried to join in; but
Ponti had disturbed her, especially with his question,
Che cosa fa adesso? She resented the uneasiness it
awoke in her.

'Are you all right, darling?' asked Sir Peter when
the session ended. 'You look tired.'

'I'm fine, Daddy, but I won't stay for tea,' she
told him, pushing back a stray lock of glossy dark
hair. 'I need a breath of fresh air after being cooped up
all day, so I think I'll take a walk along the sea front.'

'Aubrey will come with you if—'

'For heaven's sake, Daddy, I can go for a walk by

myself!' she protested with a slight frown. 'Will you be staying here for long?'

'No, I just want a word with the chappie from Edinburgh—I think I know his father. And I must congratulate that last speaker—what's his name—did you take any notes of what he said, Lucy?'

'Er—just a few. And surely it's Findlay d'Arc who's due for congratulations on the paper! Anyway, I'll see you at dinner, then, Daddy, about eight, right?'

'Make it half past, my dear. Eight o'clock at the bar. I need to go through tomorrow's programme with Aubrey, and they sit around so long here over dinner that there's no time to do any work afterwards, is there?'

He smiled as he spoke, but saw the flicker of disapproval in his daughter's violet-blue eyes.

'I don't like you having these heavy meals so late, Daddy; it's bad for your blood pressure—and so are all the brandies and cigars you're getting through here.'

The rotund baronet eyed her fondly. She was still his little girl, the pride of his life but not to be taken seriously.

'Have a heart, darling. You know what they say about when in Rome—and the same applies to Venice! Just a *little* bending of the rules while we're over here, eh?'

While we're away from Mummy's eagle eye, you mean, thought Lucy. 'I might as well pretend to agree, seeing that you never listen to a word I say, Daddy. Eight o'clock at the bar, then. Bye!'

She bent over his armchair and kissed his

cheek, aware of Portwood's eyes upon her.

'And no more than one cigar before then, right?'
She held up an adminishing forefinger.

'No, darling.'

'And *walk* back to the hotel—don't take a
water-taxi.'

'No—I mean, yes, darling.'

Lucy smiled indulgently as Portwood helped her
on with her red cashmere jacket.

'I'll keep an eye on Sir Peter for you, Lucinda.'

'Thanks, Aubrey. I know I can always rely
on you!'

With a final wave, she ran down the steps at the
entrance to Venice's municipal hospital and into the
square, Campo San Zanipolo. Turning sharply to
the right, she walked along beside a canal that led to
the sea.

It was quite true, she thought, the senior civil
servant looked after her father very well, quietly
remembering all the tiresome details that Sir Peter
was inclined to leave to others. Aubrey was always
there, dependable and discreet.

Still handsome at fifty, he had become more of a
family friend in the months following his wife's
death, and Lucy could not help noticing his growing
interest in her. He was being invited to Hallcross
Park more frequently these days, and Lucy sensed
that her parents would welcome him as a son-in-law
if she agreed.

Aubrey could offer comfort and security, a con-
tinuation of her parents' devotion; and she would
repay him by being a charming wife and hostess,
with no more humiliating experiences such as she

had undergone in the past two years. It was certainly a temptation worth considering. . .

She turned right at the sea front and walked briskly along the Fondamenta Nuove beside the Lagoon; she realised how thankful she was to get away from the conference for an hour of freedom. She needed some time to think and reflect, and where better to do so than in this most beautiful of cities?

It was a clear day in late March, warmer than in England the previous week, though a freshening breeze was whipping up from the south. Out across the shining blue water lay the green island of San Michele with Murano beyond it; so many islands and islets gleaming like jewels in the estuary, and so little time to explore, she thought.

The conference went on for the rest of the week, but Lucy had half decided to stay on over the weekend. She had a friend from student days who worked at the hospital on the Lido, and Lucy wondered whether to pay her a surprise visit.

Valeria Corsini's mother was English and she had been brought up and educated in England, training as a doctor with Lucy at St Margaret's Hospital in London. Then her parents had gone to live in Italy, and she and Lucy had lost touch.

Lucy's own career was currently at a standstill after a disastrous year at a Manchester suburban hospital which she tried not to think about; it had almost brought her to the edge of a breakdown. Now, at nearly twenty-eight, she had regained some of her self-confidence as a medical statistician in Sir Peter's ministry, but the thought of meeting Valeria again awoke mixed feelings. Who would envy whom?

Standing deep in thought, she heard a shout below her and, looking down on the water, saw two young men, scarcely out of their teens, taking off in a little sailing dinghy.

Typical Italian males, they had seen the tall, willowy girl with her dark hair streaming out behind her and were trying to get her attention to show off their expertise at hoisting the mainsail and getting their craft under way, following a zigzag course in the face of the wind.

The unrestricted sail was billowing out furiously, and the laughing youths were pulling their combined weight against it, leaning backwards almost horizontally on the windward side. They were obviously enjoying themselves, and Lucy waved to them from her safe vantage point. After all, they were in no position to pursue her right now!

Turning from the sea, she followed a narrow alleyway beside a high wall that emerged into a small square with a choice of directions. Which one would take her towards the hotel, the Albergo Cicliami, where Sir Peter and his entourage were staying?

Another narrow *calle* brought her to the edge of a quiet little canal, where green, moss-covered steps led down to the water's edge at intervals for the benefit of the small rowing craft which used it to carry vegetables, fruit and fish, to collect and deliver laundry and bring the mail to the homes and hotels that towered on either side with their wrought-iron balconies and painted shutters.

Lucy walked beside the canal for a couple of hundred yards and, turning a bend, she came upon a tiny stone bridge flanked by tubs of scarlet begonias on each side; a well-fed ginger cat dozed on the central point of the flat-topped parapet.

Lucy wished she had a camera with her to record this exquisite little corner of Venice, which must have appeared much the same a century ago, or even two, when Canaletto was painting the palaces along the Grand Canal in all their gilded glory.

The footpath ended here and Lucy crossed the bridge, following the path on the other side of the waterway. A narrow boat glided past, leaving an echo of laughter behind it, and Lucy watched it wistfully; how perfect it would be if David were here, exploring with her, hand in hand—it wouldn't matter if they lost their way, as Lucy was now beginning to suspect that she had done.

Another narrow *calle*, another *campo* dominated by an ornate medieval church, a dark passageway, and Lucy emerged once again beside the same canal as before, with the same scarlet flowers and the same ginger cat sunning himself in picturesque somnolence.

This was ridiculous, she thought crossly. She had followed a south-westerly course by the sun, and could not possibly have retraced her steps.

Yet here she undoubtedly was, lost in the maze of the Castello *sestiere* of Venice, and she would be expected at the Albergo by now. A little breathless, she leaned against the peeling pink stucco of the wall and reproached herself for not bringing a map.

The water lapped quietly against the stonework; it did not seem a likely place to hail a *motoscafo*, one of the water-taxis that busily plied for trade on the Grand Canal and the bewildering network of waterways that were the streets of this amazing city.

So, which direction should she take now? As she
considered her next move a deep voice broke in upon
her thoughts, making her start in surprise.

'This is your first visit to Venezia, yes?'

The question came from just behind her and she
spun round, not sure if it was addressed to her; she
had thought herself quite alone.

Not so, for she looked straight into the deep-set
black eyes of Dr Ponti, twinkling down at her from
his extra inches.

Taken off guard for a moment, she drew in a sharp
breath but quickly regained her poise.

'No, I have been here once before,' she replied
coolly, recalling the school trip for Italian A-level
pupils when she had been seventeen, a carefree, bossy
sixth-former.

'*Benvenuta, signorina*—welcome back!' He held
out his hand with a flourish. 'I'm Pino to my friends.
I saw you with your boss at the *conferenza* today,
and thought how much he looks like Winston
Churchill—all he needs is a top hat! Does he smoke
cigars also?'

He's got a nerve, thought Lucy, asking questions
like that! I suppose he assumes that I'm Daddy's
secretary. This man was too familiar by half, even if
he *was* just as striking at close quarters as when seen
across the Sala di Congresso. Actually considerably
more so.

And his sudden appearance was well-timed,
because he could direct her to the hotel.

'*Mi scusi, dottore*—' she began carefully, but he
fixed his dark eyes upon her in a disconcerting way

and she hesitated, giving him an opportunity to cut in and ask her name.

'Allora! Come ti chiami?' He used the familiar form of address, usually reserved for relatives and friends.

'Mi chiami Lucy Spriggs,' she replied formally. *'Sono inglese.'*

'Bella!' There was laughter in his voice. 'No need to say it, Lucia, you have ''English girl'' written all over you!'

He used the Italian form of her name, pronouncing the 'c' as 'ch' and making it sound completely different.

'Tell me, Lucia, how is it that the English delegates get all the most beautiful secretaries?' he inquired in a serious tone.

She ignored the question and pointedly looked at her watch.

'Mi scusi, dottore, ma come faccio per andare al'Albergo Cicliami, per favore?' she asked politely, hoping that he would be suitably impressed by her textbook Italian, and also get the unspoken message that she was not available for a pick-up—not even by a highly attractive Venetian doctor who clearly considered himself irresistible to women.

He was at once apologetic and put on a charming smile, giving her the benefit of his excellent teeth— apart from a slightly chipped upper incisor, she noted. And even that inexplicably added to his confounded masculine appeal.

'Va bene! I shall be happy to escort you, Signorina Lucia.'

'Oh, there is no need to—' Lucy began, but

checked herself. Directions might be hard to remember in this maze of passages, canals and bridges; she smiled, and her face took on an entirely different aspect, not lost on her companion.

'*Bellissima!* The sun comes to your eyes, Lucia. *Andiamo!*'

He reached for her hand as they walked but she deftly evaded him, hoisting her leather bag from her left shoulder to her right.

'Do you manage to come on many such trips as this?' he inquired.

'A few,' she replied. 'I was at Geneva with the World Health Organisation last year.'

'Ah, yes, the Aids convention,' he nodded, his face suddenly serious. 'Your boss is a lucky man, Lucia. Is he good to work for?'

Lucy did not want to be drawn into talk about her work, and considered it none of his business.

'Sir Peter is the ideal man for his kind of job,' she said briefly. 'And what of you, Dr Ponti? Do you enjoy general practice on the Lido?'

He glanced at her in some amusement. 'It passes the time.'

She raised her eyebrows. Perhaps he too had no wish to talk about himself or his work. They walked in silence for a minute or two, and then he spoke again.

'Forgive me, Lucia, but I see that I am not the only man who notices you. That—er—sidekick of your boss, the one who sits with him, he cannot take his eyes from you.'

Lucy was dumbstruck by such impudence. Her

expression was stony as she strode along but he plunged on, undeterred.

'But you, Lucia—you have not made up your mind about him, no?'

This was too much. Lucy's usually curving mouth hardened into a very straight line.

'Excuse me, Dr Ponti, but I have no intention of discussing my associates with you,' she said icily. 'Neither do I answer impertinent questions. Actually, I recognise where I am now, and can make my own way back to the hotel. *Buongiorno, dottore!*'

She increased her pace, her fury showing in every step. Ponti realised that she was genuinely offended, and regretted his frankness. He pursued her, his long legs soon catching up with her angry stride.

'*Mi dispiace*, Lucia, I am sorry! I did not remember how sensitive are the English,' he apologised. 'Wait, please—*allora*! What are your plans for this evening, *signorina*? Would you like a trip over to the Lido? I have a boat, and maybe I shall be permitted to offer you dinner to—er—compensate for offending you.'

He placed a hand lightly on her arm. 'Please, I really mean that, Lucia.'

His face and his voice showed his genuine regret, but Lucy was not inclined to overlook what she saw as an unpardonable insult. She shook off his hand and turned to face him, her eyes like frosted violets.

'It so happens that I *am* going over to the Lido this evening to meet a friend—' she began.

'*Meraviglioso!*' He smiled broadly. 'Then I may—'

'—but I am not in need of transport, Dr Ponti, nor your company. *Grazie!*'

They had reached a bridge and she turned away and swept across it to the other side, where he watched her disappear down the *calle* that led to the front entrance of the Albergo Cicliami. As the last whisk of her skirt flounced out of sight Ponti gave a low whistle. He was not used to such dismissive treatment from a woman.

'*Buona sera, signorina inglese,*' he muttered. '*Molte grazie.*'

CHAPTER TWO

AS SHE shampooed under the shower Lucy closed her eyes and let the water pour over her head in a long cascade, as if it could rinse away her troubled thoughts; try as she would to put the insufferable Dr Ponti out of her mind, he obstinately refused to be forgotten.

Of course he had behaved quite unpardonably, making those remarks about Aubrey and herself. What business was it of *his*, for heaven's sake, if Portwood showed his interest in her? And how *dared* Ponti challenge her about her response, her indecision about taking the next step in her life?

As she fumed with indignation, she suddenly realised why she was so resentful of Ponti's unasked-for comments: it was because they were true. She saw again his bold eyes, darkly accusing, and heard his question, *'Che cosa fa adesso?'*

For the second time that day Lucy muttered, 'Drat the man!'

Anyway, he had helped her to make a decision about this evening; with three hours to spare before dinner she had time to cross the Lagoon and take a chance on seeing Valeria at the hospital on the Lido.

Putting on a warm black sweater and leggings, Lucy tied a brightly coloured scarf over her newly washed hair and, with the red jacket and sensibly low-heeled shoes, she felt well prepared for a breezy sail on a water-bus—one of the busy *vaporetti* that journeyed up and down the Grand Canal and criss-crossed the Lagoon at all hours, calling at many islands in the archipelago and linking with the mainland.

Leaving a message for Sir Peter at the reception desk to say where she was going, Lucy made her way to the Piazza San Marco from where the *vaporetti* departed for the Lido. The famous square presented a timeless picture against the backdrop of the baroque cathedral, a renowned meeting-place for friends, families, lovers, visitors, sailors in port, priests and nuns in their black habits.

People hurried or strolled or sat, taking refreshments at the rows of tables set out on the pavement where flocks of hopeful pigeons followed the crowds and an orchestra played melodies from operas by Verdi and Puccini.

Lucy caught sight of a young man wandering disconsolately around glancing at the cathedral clock, until a pretty girl ran into his outstretched arms, explaining why she was late for their rendezvous; she seemed to be entirely forgiven in his embrace.

Lucy stifled a sigh. Venice was a city for lovers, whether meeting in the piazza or sailing in a gondola. If David Rowan were here with her—but what was the good of yearning for a man now married to someone else?

Lucy had so openly, so foolishly shown her adorbation for him, and when he'd chosen the cool, blonde sister from Maternity Lucy felt that she had become a laughing stock among the staff at Beltonshaw

General Hospital. Everything had seemed to go wrong for her after that. . .

She gave herself a little shake, and braced her slim shoulders. It was all over and done now, and self-pity would get her nowhere. After all, she had a new admirer in Aubrey Portwood, who was much more to her parents' taste than David had been, and who knew what might develop between them in the romantic atmosphere of Venice? In any case, she was determined to enjoy herself here!

A *vaporetto* was just about to leave from the landing-point and Lucy went aboard, paying her fare to a burly, black-browed boatman. As yet the annual flood of tourists was still a trickle, and her fellow passengers were mostly home-going workers or shoppers.

Her spirits rose as the boat pulled away from the shore, giving her an incomparable view of the Doge's Palace, with its Bridge of Sighs leading to the old prison. A number of vessels swarmed in the Lagoon, both sailing craft and motor-driven; half a dozen flat-bottomed and canopied boats skimmed across the water, their oarsmen shouting mock-insults to each other as they practised for a coming regatta.

When the *vaporetto* got out into deeper water the number of craft lessened and, as Lucy stood at the rail on the port side, her attention was caught by a smart motor launch with a solitary peak-capped man at the wheel, ploughing through the water in the same direction as her vessel.

Could he be Ponti? Not that she was in the least interested, of course, but she was almost sure when he came in closer. Yes, it *was* he, and he must have seen her because he was giving a wave. She turned impatiently away from the rail. Was there no escaping from the man?

A shout from two passengers at the front of the water-bus and a sudden slowing of the engines drew her attention, and she gave an involuntary cry of dismay at seeing the two youths with their sailing dinghy right in the path of the *vaporetto*. They were having trouble with the billowing mainsail, which was flapping violently and resisting all efforts to haul it in.

One of them was pulling hard on the tiller to turn the craft round before the wind and, whether an unexpected swell beneath them or a shift in the wind caused the sail to back suddenly, the boom swung round in a half-circle. Before the horrified gaze of the onlookers it struck the boy on the back of his head and swept him overboard, all in a matter of seconds.

The dinghy rocked crazily, but managed to stay upright, with the other boy clinging frantically to the mast.

As soon as the calamity took place, the shout went up from the passengers on the *vaporetto*, '*Uomo in mare!*'—Man overboard! Lucy felt the engines slowing down, and tried to keep her eyes on the youth in the water: would he manage to haul himself back on board? His companion had work enough just to keep the dinghy under control.

Passengers were calling out to him to swim to the safety of the *vaporetto*, and a roped lifebelt was hastily thrown out by the ticket-collector.

But where was he? There was no sign of a bobbing

head above the water or flailing arms reaching out. Lucy strained her eyes and then saw, to her utter dismay, an inert, white-clad body drifting; no rope, no life-belt was of use to an unconscious man, stunned by the impact of the boom on the back of his head. He was not only drifting but would drown if something was not done very soon.

'Danilo! Danilo!' Lucy heard his companion wail, and a terrible sense of helplessness seized her. The helmsman of the *vaporetto* reduced speed to zero and sounded three short blasts on the horn to warn other craft in the area. It would be dangerous to approach too close to the unconscious man, but who was there to rescue him from the sea?

Ponti! The name came into Lucy's head like a received message, and she dashed back to the port side of the deck where she had seen the motor boat, now speeding off towards the Lido.

'Pino! *Pino! Come back!*' Lucy yelled at the top of her voice, but it was the sound of the horn that caused Ponti to look back and see the frantically waving red-jacketed figure standing at the rail. She saw him change course at once, turning his boat round in a wide arc; he saw the dinghy with its solitary waving occupant, and the gesticulating passengers at the rail.

Readjusting his direction, he made for the dinghy, slowing as he neared it; he circled it carefully, following the pointing hands of the passengers. Lucy watched dry-mouthed as his eyes swept over the empty water until he spotted something white and still, drifting just below the surface.

She saw him draw alongside it, turning off the

engine. With the body to the windward side of the launch, he made two ineffectual grabs before he clutched a handful of clothing—a white woollen sweater; pulling on this, he managed to grip the youth's trouser belt with his left hand and, leaning down into the water—levering with his knees against the side—he used every ounce of his strength to haul the deadweight of the body into the cockpit.

A subdued cheer went up from the onlookers, but Lucy stood still and silent as Ponti turned on the engine and made for the *vaporetto*. The ticket-collector removed the side-rail where passengers embarked, and several men assisted Ponti to haul the apparently lifeless body of the boy onto the deck.

'*E' morto!*' cried a woman, while Lucy stood rooted to the spot, unable to move as Ponti knelt and raised the chest so that the head hung down and a gush of water dribbled from the nose and mouth. A few passengers exclaimed that the boy's chest must be full of water, but Lucy knew that the lungs took some time to fill and that this water would be mainly from the stomach.

Ponti called out for assistance, his voice sharply demanding. '*Rianimazione, pronto, pronto!*'

As if he had ordered her personally, Lucy stepped forward. She grasped the boy's jaw and thrust two fingers down his throat as far as she could. There was a further trickle of water. Ponti noted her spontaneous action, and nodded his approval.

'We must try mouth-to-mouth,' he snapped in Italian and within seconds they had lain the body straight on the deck, face upwards; Ponti knelt at one side and pulled up the chin. Like an automaton, Lucy knelt on the other side and pushed up the boy's sweater and shirt, leaning over to lay her ear against his chest—his cold, damp, silent chest.

Ponti raised his black eyebrows in an unspoken question. Was there a heartbeat? The boy could have been dead when he entered the water as a result of the blow to his head.

'I'm not sure. Perhaps,' she replied levelly. 'You start mouth-to-mouth and I'll give sternal compression.'

He made no comment but went straight into the drill of artificial respiration: the kiss of life. With the boy's head well back, Ponti pinched his nose between the thumb and forefinger of his left hand then, taking a deep breath, he leaned over and fastened his lips entirely over the boy's limply gaping mouth. And he blew breath from his own lungs into the other's motionless chest. There was not a flicker of response.

As Ponti sat back on his heels, panting from the effort needed to inflate another person's lungs, Lucy felt like a spectator watching herself as she now leaned over the boy and placed her hands over his heart, right hand upon left, palms downwards.

One-two-three-four-five, she counted silently, and on each number she pushed down firmly, giving the heart five short squeezes and hoping that it would be stimulated to contract.

When she sat back on her heels, Ponti inclined forward again and repeated his attempt to force air into the boy's lungs. This time Lucy noticed a very faint rise of the chest. A woman cried out *'Viva! Respira!'* but Lucy knew that it only proved that air was getting into the lungs—the boy could still be dead. She tilted over the body again and repeated the five short, sharp pushes down; then she sat back while Ponti made a third attempt to inflate the lungs, and again the chest rose.

Lucy continued to work automatically, alternating sternal compression with Ponti's mouth-to-mouth breathing. After sixteen repetitions she ceased to count but simply prayed silently that there would be some sort of a response soon—before exhaustion claimed the first-aiders.

Ponti was red in the face and his hair stuck in jet-black clumps to his sweating forehead; he panted rapidly during the brief intervals between insufflations. It was surely hopeless! Yet as long as Ponti was able to continue so must she persevere with her sternal pressure on the heart, though the likelihood of success was diminishing with every second that passed.

And then, as she sat back and Ponti leaned forward to try once again, they both saw the chest give a sharp, spontaneous rise, while at the same time there was a choking sound in the boy's throat. His eyelids fluttered, and again a cry of *'Respira!'* went up.

Lucy briefly caught Ponti's eye as a wordless thought was exchanged. Moving in unison, they put their arms under the boy's shoulders and pulled him up to a sitting position on the deck. He belched, and vomited more water. Lucy thumped his back. 'Give a cough, Danilo,' she ordered.

Ponti repeated, *'Tossisci!'*

Before their eyes life returned to the half-drowned young man, though his nose and ears remained blue. He shuddered and gasped, focusing his eyes upon

Lucy—who began to remove his wet clothes and wrap him in blankets from the boat's emergency store. He moaned feebly and clung to her while Ponti gently examined the swelling on the back of his head: the skull did not appear to be fractured, but an X-ray would be needed to check.

The journey to the Lido was resumed and the helmsman used his radio to summon the police rescue control to the other youth, marooned on the dinghy in the gathering dusk, and also to tow in Ponti's motor boat. Using his doctor's mobile telephone, Ponti called the hospital on the Lido to send an ambulance to the landing-point at Santa Maria Elisabetta, where they very quickly arrived.

The shivering boy was placed on a stretcher by two attendants who greeted Ponti as 'Dr Pino'. He caught Lucy's eye and smiled.

'I'll go with him to Pronto Soccorso—you are free to enjoy your evening now,' he told her. However, Danilo had other ideas.

'Non lasciarmi, signorina!' he pleaded—Don't leave me! And Lucy could not do so; she got into the ambulance and sat down beside the boy, holding his hand.

'Dov'è Giorgio—lo mio amico?' Where is Giorgio, my friend?

She glanced at Ponti who replied with a sympathetic shrug, and she tried to reassure the boy that his friend was being rescued and would probably be brought to the hospital.

He gave her a wobbly smile. 'You and the doctor saved my life,' he said in Italian.

The doctor. . . On the *vaporetto* Lucy had heard

the boatmen and passengers expressing their relief at
the presence of a doctor and, of course, they'd meant
Ponti. Nobody had known the qualifications of the
woman who had assisted him with resuscitation.

It took only a few minutes to reach the Ospedale
Al Mare, the seaside hospital that served the Lido.
In the *pronto soccorso*—or first-aid department—
Lucy felt herself caught up again in a familiar bust-
ling world, the patients waiting on trolleys or
wheelchairs for X-rays and laboratory tests.

She marvelled at the similarity of hospitals everywhere, whether old or new, large or small: the
atmosphere, the very smell was universal. She
noticed that Ponti seemed to be very much at home,
and known to everybody.

'Hi, Pino, who have you picked up this time?'
asked the casualty officer with a grin, and Lucy was
uncomfortably aware of his glance in her direction
as well as at Danilo. He soon decided to admit Danilo
for overnight observation, and as the trolley was
about to be wheeled away to a medical ward two
police officers arrived with a white-faced Giorgio,
the youth left on the dinghy.

Ponti was told that his motor boat was safely
moored at the landing-point and that the police
needed to take down some details of the accident.

While the two friends hugged each other in an
emotional reunion, Giorgio's eyes lit up at the sight
of Lucy.

'*Signorina!* You are the girl we saw on the
Fondamente Nuove!' he exclaimed in Italian.
'*Bellissima!*'

'Leave her to me, Giorgio,' warned his friend with

a weak grin. 'It's my life she saved, so I have first claim.'

With such encouraging signs of recovery, Lucy felt free to slip away quietly to the reception desk and inquire about Valeria.

'Dr Corsini? She is not on duty this evening,' replied the porter, looking at the duty roster. 'You can leave a message for when she comes in tomorrow.'

Lucy hastily scribbled a note to Valeria, giving her hotel telephone number and inviting her former fellow student to ring and arrange a meeting before the end of the Venice convention.

And now there was nothing for her to do but return to the landing-point at Santa Maria Elisabetta and get on a *vaporetto* for San Marco and the Albergo Cicliami, where her father would be waiting for her to join him at dinner.

She stood uncertainly at the hospital entrance, and found that her knees were trembling. She steadied herself against the wall and closed her eyes, telling herself not to be silly—that there was no need for alarm now. Danilo was safe and recovering well, and she had given what assistance she could in the emergency.

So why did she feel so drained? And so cold? To her dismay, she realised that she was crying, and that the porter on Reception was giving her a curious look. And try as she would, she could not stop; she was standing here crying in public—how simply awful!

She did not notice the tall figure dashing out of Pronto Soccorso; she only heard him speaking breathlessly when he reached her side.

'Lucia! I have searched for you—where have you been? Why, Lucia, you are—'

And the next thing she knew was that two strong arms were around her and a deep voice was murmuring close to her ear. Held against his padded jacket, she was surrounded by a tremendous sense of warmth—a haven of security in a cold and precarious world.

'It's all right, *cara mia*, I have you safe, don't cry—*sei sicura con me*!' he assured her then, in a more teasing tone, he added softly, 'Hey! After all that heroism you should be feeling proud!'

The comfort of his presence was overwhelming. Strength seemed to flow from his body into hers, and instinctively she turned within the circle of his arms and buried her face against his jacket, stifling her sobs. He tightened his hold on her, and for a few moments she weakly gave herself up to the bliss of being held closely while his reassuring words soothed her.

The extraordinary thought came into Lucy's head that she would be happy to spend the rest of her life in the safety of these arms, resting upon this broad shoulder; her sobs quietened into sighs, and she drew some deep breaths.

'You are better now, yes, *cara mia*?'

Lucy slowly raised her head from its comfortable place in the hollow of his shoulder. Reality swept over her like a dash of cold water—heavens above! What on earth was she doing here in this strange place with a man she hardly knew?

She lowered her eyes as a scarlet blush spread up over her face and neck; even her ears reddened with the sheer embarrassment of the situation. She simply could not raise her tear-stained face to meet those twinkling eyes now looking down on her discomfiture. And *this* after the way she had spoken to him earlier. . . Lucy could have wished the ground to open and swallow her on the spot.

'Dr Ponti, I—I'm sorry,' she managed to say in a small, shaky voice, very different from the dismissive tone she had used earlier that day.

'Sorry? For what? Listen, Lucia, you were wonderful! I could not believe my eyes when you knelt down and began that cardiac compression—and it worked, did it not? I doubt if I could have brought him round on my own—I had no breath left!' He laughed ruefully at the recollection. 'Look, the *polizia* are offering to drive me back to where my *Isabella* waits for me.'

'*Who?*' asked Lucy in bewilderment.

'The *motoscafo*—my boat! They've brought her in, and the dinghy. *Avanti!*'

Taking her arm, he led her to the waiting police car and helped her into the back seat. The two officers smiled and offered their congratulations to her as they drove back to the landing-point. Ponti kept his arm firmly around her shoulders during the short journey, and she made no objection—it was so warm and comforting.

On reaching their destination, Ponti again took her arm.

'I'll take you back to the mainland, but first you need treatment for shock—a reviving drink and something to eat,' he informed her, whisking her into a bar close to the landing-stage and ordering a brandy and a wedge of *panettone*, the delectable sweet confection loved by Italians.

The fiery brandy certainly had a reviving effect on Lucy, who sipped it gratefully.

'Another?' he offered.

'Heavens, no! I shall be *drunk*,' she protested, laughing. 'And, honestly, I must get back to my hotel.'

'Where did you learn your first aid?' he asked curiously. 'I do not expect such professional technique from a secretary!'

Lucy did not want to tell him the truth about herself—that she was a qualified doctor; that would involve further questions that she had no wish to answer, particularly to this disturbing stranger who had apparently been impressed by her performance on the *vaporetto*. So she replied with a half-truth.

'It was part of a course I took,' she said lightly. 'Actually, I work in medical statistics for the Ministry of Health.'

'It must have been a very good course,' he observed, and Lucy hastily took another bite of her *panettone*.

'This is absolutely delicious, though it must be terribly fattening,' she murmured, avoiding his questioning look.

'What happened to your plans for this evening?' he asked. 'Did not you say you had an arrangement?'

She lowered her eyes, remembering her ungracious refusal to have dinner with him.

'The friend I was hoping to meet is not—er, free this evening. And, besides, after all the trauma I don't feel very sociable. My fa—my friends will be expecting me back for dinner,' she said a little awkwardly. She could see that he did not look convinced by this evasion, but must have decided that it was no concern of his for he did not pursue the subject.

'Right, Lucia, if you are ready, we can leave now. You are happy to cross the Lagoon in my little *motoscafo*, yes?'

She was impressed by the comfort of the trim motor launch—smart and shiny in appearance and speedily efficient as she cut through the now darkened water, throwing up a smooth wave on each side of her prow. The lights of Venice beckoned magically across the Lagoon, and Lucy was almost sorry when they arrived at his regular mooring on the Riva degli Schiavoni. He locked *Isabella* to a capstan, expertly tying the mooring-ropes.

'Is she staying here overnight?' asked Lucy.

'No, I shall return to the Lido—she is berthed there,' he replied, and Lucy remembered that he had a general practice on the elongated island that guarded the harbour. Everybody had seemed to know him—from the police to the ambulance crew—and the thought occurred to Lucy that he might know Valeria Corsini, in which case her little deception would be revealed to him sooner or later.

But I'll be home by then, she thought, and won't have to hear his reaction!

He took her arm and led her through two narrow *calli* and over the bridge to the street entrance of the Albergo Cicliami. Lucy's heart sank when she saw Aubrey Portwood standing on the steps, smoking a cigarette and looking anxiously up and down the ancient cobbled street. His face registered unconcealed relief when he saw Lucy.

'Thank God, Lucinda!' he exclaimed with none of his usual composure. 'I've been trying to reassure your father that you'd return from the Lido in time for dinner, but he's been very worried. My dear, why on earth did you take yourself off across the Lagoon on your own?'

His voice was sharp with his own anxiety, and the sight of Ponti's amused grin did nothing to improve matters. Lucy felt abashed at having caused her father worry.

'It's quite all right, Aubrey, there's no need to fuss, honestly,' she apologised. 'Actually, I haven't been alone—you'll remember Dr Ponti from this afternoon? He has kindly brought me back in his motor boat.' She turned to her escort, who held out his hand.

'Delighted to acquaint myself with you, Audrey,' he said in a friendly way, though Lucy cringed at the mispronunciation. 'Here is your secretary safe and well after reviving a drowned man!'

Portwood was clearly in no mood for tales of adventure.

'Secretary? What are you talking about?' he snapped. 'Her father has been very upset by her absence, and—and so have I. Did *you* persuade her to—?'

'Wait a minute, Audrey,' cut in Ponti. 'Did you say "father"? The one with the face of Churchill?'

He turned to Lucy, who rolled up her eyes in embarrassment.

'Lucia! You did not tell me that he was your *father*!'

'I'm sorry, Dr Ponti,' she shrugged, wondering how best to ease the awkward situation and aware of

the tension between the two men. 'Perhaps I had
better introduce Mr Aubrey Portwood, private secretary to my father, Sir Peter Hallcross-Spriggs.'

'Who is a Member of Parliament and junior
Minister of Health,' added Portwood loftily.

'*O mio Dio*!' gasped Ponti, clapping his hand to
his mouth. 'And Lucia—'

'Lucia nothing!' barked Portwood. 'She is the
Honourable Dr Lucinda Hallcross-Spriggs, his
daughter.'

'Oh, Aubrey, for goodness' sake!' protested Lucy,
hardly able to look at Ponti who gave a long whistle
and bowed towards her.

'If you had only told me, honourable *dottoressa*,
I would have worn my *diadema* instead of this
sailing cap.'

In spite of her exasperation Lucy could hardly keep
a straight face, while Portwood continued to glare at
the cheerfully unconcerned Italian. It was surely time
to bring the unfortunate scene to a dignified con-
clusion.

'We had better say goodnight now, Dr Ponti,' she
said in her best hostess manner. 'I know you have
to get back to the Lido, so—'

She saw the gentle mockery in his piercing dark
eyes, and did not finish the sentence.

'So—*buona notte, dottoressa*,' he responded.
'And thank you for a most—er—enlightening
evening. As I have said already, you were wonderful—*meravigliosa! Ciao*, Audrey!'

Lucy stared after his retreating back with very
mixed feelings indeed.

'My dear Lucinda, I'm sorry if I spoke out of turn,'

Aubrey apologised, his usually impassive features suffused with a dark flush of annoyance. 'But your father—'

Lucy cut him short.

'Thank you, Aubrey. Sometimes I wish that you and Daddy would notice that I have grown up.'

And with that she marched past him into the hotel to confront Sir Peter's relief and reproaches.

Men! Really, they were impossible. . .

Yet as she lay in bed that night and reflected on the unforeseen happenings of the day, it was the memory of Ponti's praise for her expertise and presence of mind in the emergency that gave her the most satisfaction. A young life had been saved, and what mattered more than that?

CHAPTER THREE

'DO YOU feel up to attending this morning, darling?' asked Sir Peter, standing in the doorway of Lucy's room. 'Let me ask them to send your breakfast up to you.'

Lucy sighed. 'Of course I shall attend, Daddy, it's what I've come here for. I'll see you downstairs at breakfast, right?'

'But after all the stress of last night, Lucinda, you need time to recover,' he protested anxiously.

Lucy tried to keep the impatience out of her voice.

'Daddy, dear, *do* go away and let me get dressed. And stop fussing over me like an old mother hen— *please*?'

Hearing the finality of her tone, the baronet reluctantly obeyed—to his daughter's relief.

In fact, Lucy did indeed feel unsettled after her adventure of the previous evening; her mirror reflected pale cheeks and dark smudges under her eyes—all the more reason for putting on extra make-up and entering the Sala di Congresso promptly at nine, she thought. Daddy was a dear, of course, but it was infuriating to be treated like a pampered schoolgirl who could skip lessons if she wished. It made her feel as if her presence here was not necessary at all.

Well, *was* it? asked that persistent voice in her head again. Last night she had not even admitted to being a doctor—and look where her foolish deception had led! She went hot and cold at the memory of Aubrey's pompous words to Ponti, who had at least proved himself to be a competent practising doctor, and he had been incredibly kind when she had behaved so ridiculously at the hospital. What must he think of her now?

She brushed her thick hair back into an elegant swirl and secured it with a tortoiseshell comb. She would face Ponti today with calm courtesy, not revealing any of the turmoil he had stirred up inside her. She removed the crystal drop earrings she had put on in favour of plain gold studs, as being more businesslike.

She did not know whether to be glad or sorry when the morning session passed with no sign of Ponti.

Perhaps he was no longer needed as a presenter of other men's papers and had gone back to his practice on the Lido, in which case she would not see him again so there was no problem—and Lucy's spirits fell so flat that she had to make an effort to be civil to Aubrey Portwood when he brought her coffee halfway through the morning, with a choice of English newspapers. He sat beside her and politely inquired how she felt.

'The reason I'm asking, Lucinda, is that I'd like to take you and Sir Peter out to dinner at L'Usignolo Argento this evening,' he said, smiling. 'With Miss Elstone, of course.'

Of course, thought Lucy, so that Meg can chat to Daddy and Aubrey can have me to himself.

'I've mentioned it to Sir Peter,' went on Portwood, 'and he thinks it would be a good idea, provided that you feel up to it. So shall I book a table for four at, say, eight o'clock?'

Lucy gave him a cool smile. 'That would be very nice.'

'Good! Thank you, Lucinda,' he answered with satisfaction. 'If you'll excuse me, I'll book it now.'

As he was getting up a white-jacketed buffet attendant brought Lucy a mobile telephone.

'*Mi scusi, signorina*—there is a call for you.'

The voice in her ear brought an immediate smile to Lucy's face.

'Valeria! Oh, hi! How are you? I missed you last night at your hospital—'

Portwood hovered at a discreet distance while the two former friends exchanged greetings, but heard every word Lucy said.

'Yes, I'd love to meet you this evening, Valeria. The only thing is, I've been asked to—er—'

She looked at Portwood, and he at once understood.

'My dear Lucinda, please include your friend in our party tonight,' he offered without hesitation.

Lucy covered the mouthpiece. 'Are you sure?' she whispered. L'Usignolo Argento was as expensive as it was exclusive.

'Certainly. I shall be delighted.'

'That's very generous of you, Aubrey. Hallo, Val—listen, I wonder if you could come over and join a little dinner party at eight? Daddy's private secretary has just arranged it—yes, Val, he insists that you come too—oh, fine, that will be super!'

And so it was settled that Valeria would come to the hotel at six for a drink and a chat before getting ready in Lucy's room to go out to dinner. Lucy's spirits rose considerably. With Valeria in the party, she would not be monopolised by Aubrey. She was not at all sure that she wanted to get further involved with him just yet; she needed time.

Her experiences of the previous night had given her a new perspective on her life, and she could sense changes on the way. Dared she hope for a return to practising as a doctor in some capacity? Perhaps a heart-to-heart talk with Valeria would help.

Lucy was aware of a pang of envy as she considered her old friend's lifestyle. Working with patients, discussing case histories with colleagues and trying out different treatments appeared much more rewarding than her job in the Ministry.

With no financial pressure there was less incentive to return to the profession for which she had spent six years training, only to lose her nerve two years later. After the bitter disappointment over David Rowan, closely followed by a professional crisis— and Lucy shuddered at the memory of *that* terrible ordeal—she had been only too willing to escape to the sanctuary of Hallcross Park, where her parents had showered her with sympathy and indignation against the Beltonshaw Health Authority.

The peace of the Wiltshire countryside had restored her confidence to some extent, and now she was quite happily employed in a nine-to-five job that enabled her to come on these sort of trips with Daddy. She knew that many of her friends envied her, but. . .

Che cosa fa adesso? asked that voice again: what are you doing now? And she remembered Ponti's piercing black eyes—and that extraordinary interlude last night when she had wept in his arms outside the Ospedale Al Mare.

Lunch with her father brought the news that the dinner party had expanded further.

'Delighted to hear that you've asked Dr Corsini over, darling,' said the genial baronet. 'And Aubrey has asked that young chappie we met on Monday—what's his name, the one who works here.'

'Dr Scogliera, the fair-haired one in Radiotherapy?' asked Lucy.

'That's the one, a nice young fellow. That'll make up a good balanced party of six—couldn't be better, eh?'

Lucy frowned. She had a shrewd idea that Portwood had deliberately equalised the numbers in order to partner Valeria with the young doctor, thus freeing herself to be his partner at the table. He was determined not to be left out of the running, that much was clear.

If I was to ask Valeria to bring a friend, she thought with a flash of irritation, Aubrey would find another guest of the opposite sex, and so it could go on. She wondered just how many guests he would be prepared to pay for.

Oh, well, it would be a chance to savour Venetian night life at its highest level, for L'Usignolo was known as a haunt of the international set who attended the operas at La Fenice and the plays at the Teatro Goldoni.

After lunch there was half an hour to spare before the convention reassembled at two, and Lucy escaped out of the imposing front entrance for a breath of air and privacy in the wide square, dominated by the church of St John and St Paul.

Three children were happily bouncing a ball against the towering church wall in the sunshine and, when Lucy saw an ice-cream vendor on the opposite side of the square, she could not resist treating them and herself to well-filled cones, much to their delight. Standing beside the huge equestrian statue in the middle of the square, she felt a little self-conscious with the dripping cone in her hand. It needed to be demolished fairly quickly!

The sun was warm on her face and arms and Lucy gradually felt herself relaxing in the beauty of this amazing city, built upon the sea a thousand years ago and still standing. How she would love to stay on here after the convention, she thought, to explore the past glories of Venice, preserved for present admiration—and perhaps inspiration? It would mean cancelling her flight on Saturday, and she'd have to find somewhere more modest than the Albergo Cicliami to stay; perhaps Valeria might know of a place. She leaned against the railing around the statue, and let her imagination wander. . .

'You wait for someone, *dottoressa*?'

She jerked herself upright, and there was Pino Ponti smiling down at her as she licked an ice-cream cone in a public place. This would never have happened at home!

'*Buongiorno, dottore,*' she said, adjusting her expression accordingly.

'I see that you have discovered the *gelato*. It is good, yes?' He nodded towards her half-eaten cone.

'Yes—*si, è delizioso,*' she agreed. 'And how are

you today, *dottore*? I didn't see you at the convention this morning,' she added, and then immediately wished she had not given the impression that she had looked out for him.

'No, I had other business in the hospital,' he said. 'My services were not required at the *conferenza*.'

Lucy wondered what he could have been doing in the Ospedale Civile, but would not have dreamed of asking.

'I wonder how Danilo is feeling today?' she ventured. 'Discharged by now, I expect.'

'Probably. I hope they have given him antibiotic cover,' he remarked. 'The waters of the Lagoon are known for a high level of pollution from too much— er—*acqua di scolo*—effluent. Danilo's worst danger now is from infection.'

Lucy nodded, aware of the dark eyes scanning her face closely and roving over her slim figure; she lowered her eyes, and the corners of his mouth lifted in a half-smile.

'And how are *you* today, *dottoressa*?'

'*Sto bene, grazie,*' she said firmly. 'I'm fine. Danilo was very lucky that you were on hand when he went overboard,' she continued quickly, not wanting the conversation to take a personal turn. 'I shan't forget the way you pulled him out of the water into your boat—I was afraid you would fall in as well.'

'So was I!' Disconcertingly, he put out a long finger and touched the tip of her nose. '*Gelato,*' he grinned, and she realised that she must have a blob of ice-cream on her face.

'Oh, heavens!' She hastily opened her bag and took out a tissue. How simply humiliating! He looked on in amusement as she wiped her nose and mouth, and she found that it was impossible to stand on her dignity while this man was around. There was something about him that cut through all her defences, and there was a warmth—as she had discovered last night—that radiated from him like an aura. Why not accept his easy friendliness at face value?

Then he asked the inevitable question.

'Lucia, why did you let me think you were a secretary, and did not tell me you are a doctor, no? It put me at a disadvantage with—er—Audrey.'

He was still smiling, and there seemed no need to make a big issue of it.

'His name is *Aubrey*,' she corrected, 'Mr Aubrey Portwood. As for me, it hardly seemed important with a man's life at stake. Who cares about status at a time like that? You got Danilo breathing again; that's what matters, surely?'

'Correction, Lucia—*we* got him breathing. Without your sternal compression, I doubt he would have revived, no? I tell you, I thought he was dead on the deck.'

'So did I,' she confessed with a shiver.

'But you did a great job, Lucia.'

'Correction, Pino—*we* did a great job, right?'

He threw back his head and laughed aloud, his open-necked shirt revealing a triangle of healthily glowing flesh on which a few black hairs curled. How devastatingly handsome this man was! She lowered her gaze in sudden confusion, and looked at her watch.

'Time to go back to the hall, I think.'

'Ah, yes. Again, I shall not be able to attend for the afternoon session. I have a— *O mio Dio!*'

Looking over her shoulder, he broke off in mid-sentence and, with a complete change of mood, he left her side and held out his arms to a slightly built blonde girl coming from the hospital. Lucy saw her slide thankfully into his embrace, and also saw the anxiety on his face as he held the girl like some precious object that he feared to lose. Lucy heard them greet each other in Italian.

'Gabriella, *cara mia*!'

'Pino! I looked for you—'

'Forgive me, I did not think you would be through so soon, or I would have waited.'

He released her, and Lucy saw her look up innocently into his face. Her eyes were large and deep blue, and her skin had a porcelain transparency; silky fair hair waved softly back into a topknot, tied with a blue gauze scarf. As well as being thoroughly taken aback, Lucy was sure she had seen this girl before somewhere.

'How did you get on with the professor?' asked Ponti.

'Very well, he is so charming! The blood and bone marrow has been taken, and I must attend him again on Monday,' answered the girl. 'He will then tell me if I need treatment in hospital.'

'I see. Yes. Good,' he murmured but a shadow fell across his face, as if he thought the news anything but good. Lucy felt that she should not be listening, and began to move away.

The girl saw her and called out to her to stay.

'*Mi perdoni, signorina, per interrompare!*'

Lucy hesitated, and Ponti collected himself to introduce them.

'Lucia, this is Gabriella Rasi, a dear friend who is staying on the Lido for a while. Gabriella, meet Dr Lucia—er—Spriggs from England, who is attending the convention this week.'

'*Buongiorno*, Gabriella,' responded Lucy at once.

'*Buongiorno*, Lucia!'

The unaffected sweetness in the girl's smile went straight to Lucy's heart. There was a tender fragility about her, as if a puff of wind might carry her away, and all at once Lucy remembered her face.

'Gabriella—didn't I see you in a film about the life of Vivaldi? You were an orphan girl, one of his pupils—'

The girl's huge eyes widened still further.

'*La Figlia della Pietà*? And did you like it?'

'Yes, very much, especially you—I remember I cried when you renounced your lover to become a nun,' recalled Lucy, and then checked herself abruptly as she saw Ponti's frown; Gabriella must be very special to him and, from what she had heard, there seemed to be some anxiety about her health.

'You are very kind, Lucia—is she not, Pino?' smiled the girl, turning from one to the other. 'It is thanks to Pino that I am here today for an appointment with the *professore del' oncologia*,' she explained in a friendly, confiding way, but Lucy saw that Pino looked sombre and felt that she should not intrude upon what might be a delicate matter.

'I really must go now,' she said. 'It has been a real pleasure to meet you in person, Gabriella.'

'I feel that you are a friend, Lucia, and we shall

meet again,' said the actress with conviction, and for a moment there was silence—a pause in which Lucy was also aware of a strange rapport between herself and this girlfriend of Ponti's.

'Come, *cara mia*,' he said, 'I will take you across the Lagoon to be properly cared for. And if any idiot falls in today it will be his bad luck,' he added grimly with a nod towards Lucy, his usually generous mouth compressed to a thin line. He tucked Gabriella's arm under his, and with a final *'Arrivederci!'* to Lucy he led her away.

A melancholy mood descended on Lucy as she returned to the Sala di Congresso. Gabriella's trusting, childlike face stayed in her mind and the words *midollo sternale*, which she had overheard, bothered her; bone-marrow samples meant that the girl was being tested for a serious form of anaemia, though she was clearly unaware of the possible gravity of her condition, while Ponti was having to hide his own fears.

Were the pair in love? Lucy wondered. If so, Ponti still felt free to flirt with other women—including herself! She had better not indulge in any daydreams about being held in his arms at the Ospedale Al Mare. She was a mere visitor, a passing encounter, whereas the sweet-faced actress obviously meant a great deal to him. Remembering his stricken face when he heard Gabriella's report, she pictured him anxiously awaiting the results of the laboratory tests on Monday.

Looking up, she caught Aubrey's questioning smile and gave a little shrug. It was useless to speculate about Ponti and his actress friend when she should be taking stock of her own life and future.

At the end of the session Sir Peter was conversing with two Dutch delegates over tea, and told Lucy to go back to the hotel with Aubrey and Meg; he would join her later.

'And no swanning off to the Lido, darling!' he warned, waving a forefinger.

'Don't worry, I shall take good care of her, sir,' said Aubrey, drawing her arm through his with a proprietory air, while a stony-faced Meg Elstone picked up her briefcase and turned her back on them, murmuring that she had letters to post.

'What on earth's the matter with that girl?' sighed Lucy. 'Every time I try to talk to her, she just cold-shoulders me.'

'Missing her boyfriend, I expect,' smiled Aubrey. 'Now, Lucinda, satisfy a dream of mine and let's take a gondola back to the hotel!'

'Aren't they very expensive?' asked Lucy doubtfully.

'Lucinda, dear, just this once indulge a lonely man who asks nothing more than to sail in a gondola on the Grand Canal of Venice with a beautiful girl,' he pleaded, his head close to hers.

He was making his extravagance into a favour for her to bestow, and how could she refuse? She let him lead her down the weathered stone steps to a row of black-painted gondolas moored to the vertical striped poles that were so much a part of the Venice scene. The moustachioed gondolier in his wide-brimmed straw hat handed her down into the chair seat, where Aubrey took his place beside her.

They were soon poled out into the centre of the canal, from where the magnificent palaces that lined both banks could be seen to the best advantage. Aubrey pointed out the buildings of particular interest.

'There's the Palazzo Justinian where Wagner wrote *Tristan and Isolde*,' he said, 'and over there—'

Lucy found it impossible to take in so much information, interesting though it was. She nodded vaguely as she gazed at the magnificent succession of façades, with their columns, carvings, graceful arched windows and balustrades on both sides of the famous waterway, and felt that she should be enjoying every moment.

Yet there was a certain awkwardness, a sense of something not being quite right: gondolas were for lovers, and Lucy knew that she was not in love with the man now beside her. Respect, trust and appreciation of his reliability, yes—there was no doubting his affection, his willingness to cherish and protect her.

So why could she not just accept what he had to offer, and thank Heaven for a good man's devotion? Her parents approved and, apart from the difference in their ages, he was right for her in every way.

His arm had gently enclosed her shoulders as they reclined in the cushioned chair, and it was a perfect setting for romance, but Lucy was not sorry when they turned off into the canal that brought them to the landing-stage at the Albergo Cicliami. She thanked him for the ride, but declined a drink at the hotel bar; it was nearly time for Valeria Corsini to arrive.

The two young women embraced like long-lost sisters.

'Honourable Lucinda! You haven't changed at all—still the same aristocratic air!'

'Oh, do shut up, Val! You know I never use the Hon! Come on, I'll take you to a nice little bar where we can have a good natter away from Daddy's entourage.'

Laughing, they hurried along the narrow *calle* and took their places at a secluded table near the counter where Venetians met after work.

'Who exactly are we meeting tonight, Lucy?'

'We're being wined and dined by Aubrey Portwood, Daddy's private secretary, my dear!'

'Ooh! Sounds impressive—and have I got to entertain dear old Sir Peter while you touch feet under the table with our host?'

'Don't be ridiculous!' scolded Lucy, though in fact she was overjoyed at this reunion with her high-spirited friend. 'Daddy's typist, Meg Elstone, will be with us, and a Dr Scogliera from Radioterapia.'

'Ah, I know Gianni Scogliera,' said Valeria, her eyes brightening. 'We send a few patients over for radiotherapy—there's a funny little nursing-home on the Lido, run by an impoverished countess, where some of them stay between treatments. It's nicer than being in a hospital ward and, besides, we need the beds. So many wards have been closed due to cut-backs.' She sighed. 'But I want to hear all about *you*, Lucy. How did you get to be at the convention?'

Lucy glanced down into her coffee. 'Actually, I'm here with Daddy as a statistician, Val. It seems to suit me better than the hospital scene.'

'Really? Didn't you go to somewhere in

Manchester after graduating?' asked Valeria in surprise.

'Yes—and quite honestly I'd rather forget about it,' replied Lucy, avoiding her friend's eyes.

'We're a long way from Manchester now,' said Valeria gently. 'Want to tell Auntie Val what happened?'

And all of a sudden Lucy discovered that she was thankful for a chance to confide in an understanding woman friend of her own age, one who had shared her medical training days.

'Just about everything went wrong at Beltonshaw General, Val. There was this obstetrics registrar—I made a complete fool of myself over him, but I honestly thought that he was interested and he seemed to return my feelings.

'I invited him to stay for a few days at Hallcross Park, and it just didn't work out. He and Mummy rubbed each other up the wrong way, for a start— she was taken aback when he talked about his upbringing in the East End of London; it turned out that he came from a real problem family.

'I admired him for rising above his background, but—well, all of a sudden he got engaged to one of the sisters in Maternity, and that was that. I was so sure that he felt the same way as I did, and everybody knew I was crazy about him. It—it was shattering—'

Her voice trembled, and Valeria touched her hand in silent sympathy.

'And then—what happened after that? Did you finish your obstetrics and gynaecology house job?'

'Yes, but it was sheer hell. It was a busy department, and when I was on call I sometimes worked all day and most of the night. There were times when I panicked and just couldn't cope with the physical and emotional demands, especially after losing David. We still had to work together, you see—I was even invited to the wedding but, of course, I didn't go.'

'Oh, Lucy, you poor love!'

'And then something really ghastly happened, Val, just too awful for words. There was this pregnant diabetic woman—not just gestational diabetes, she'd had it since childhood—and you know how it can go completely haywire in pregnancy; she was always going into hypoglycaemia, and every time the physicians lowered her insulin she'd go the other way—*hyper*glycaemic. She spent weeks in the antenatal ward.'

Lucy hesitated, and Valeria said, 'Go on.'

'She went into a hypo one night at around 2 a.m., and the night nurse couldn't rouse her so rang for me. I was fast asleep—it had been one hell of a day in the delivery unit and gynae theatre. The phone woke me, and I said I'd be down right away.'

'I can guess what's coming,' said Valeria quietly. 'You turned over and fell asleep again. It's happened before. And when the nurse rang you again—'

'She didn't. She rang the registrar—David Rowan,' replied Lucy in a flat, dull tone. 'He rushed to the ward and took a blood sample, which he put straight through the glycometer. The sugar level was non-existent, and he gave a stat dose of intravenous dextrose five per cent. She came round at once, as they do, but of course she was a bit disorientated and upset, and all the other patients were awake.'

Lucy bit her lip and tears sprung to her eyes.

'Try not to get upset, Lucy dear,' said Valeria gently. 'I'm listening, and everything you say is confidential. Did David say anything to you?'

Lucy took a tissue from her bag and wiped her eyes before continuing.

'No. I suddenly woke up in a panic and rushed down to the ward in my dressing-gown and slippers, by which time the emergency was over and David was talking to the nurses in the office over coffee. He was very sweet about it, but the patient guessed that he'd been sent for because I hadn't come when called.

'She told her husband about it, and he made a complaint to the Beltonshaw Health Authority—so, of course, there had to be an independent inquiry.

'Oh, Val, it was a nightmare—David had to give evidence and so did the night nurses, and in the end I was acquitted of professional negligence because no actual harm had been caused, plus the fact that I'd been on duty for eighteen hours.

'So I got off with a reprimand, and apologised to the patient and to the health authority—but the *Manchester Evening News* got hold of the story from somewhere, and it was all across the headlines. Of course I was a nervous wreck by then—oh, Val!' She choked back a sob.

'My dear Lucy, what a terrible time you've been through,' murmured Valeria, shaking her head. 'And then?'

'I completed my six months' contract for obs and gynae, and applied for a housemanship in Paediatrics.'

'That was brave, Lucy.'

'But the Beltonshaw Health Authority refused to take out a new contract with me, and so I—I finished. I went home and just collapsed—couldn't do a thing for weeks—and then Daddy got me this job at the Ministry in the Statistics Office. I've always been fairly good at maths and it's quite interesting, really. Anyway, I've landed on my feet again, with no harm done.

'The patient eventually had a Caesarean section at thirty-seven weeks, and everything was fine—a healthy baby girl. That's enough of me, Val—now let's talk about you!'

But Valeria Corsini was quite horrified by Lucy's account of her humiliating experiences at Beltonshaw and the disastrous effect on her career. She remembered Lucy as a rather high-handed medical student at St Margaret's, where her upper-class accent had not endeared her to the nursing staff. Sympathetic as she was, Valeria privately wondered if her friend's misfortunes had also had some beneficial effect: she seemed so much nicer now!

'Forgive me, Lucy, but I think you should get away from your parents,' she said bluntly. 'They spoil you!'

Lucy flushed. It was exactly what she herself had been thinking recently. One way would be to marry Aubrey, but what other options were there?

'I don't know, Val. Right now I'm just thankful to be here in Venice,' she sighed.

'Why don't you stay for a while?' asked Valeria on an impulse. 'You could do with a complete change of scene.' And to get away from that doting mummy and daddy, she added to herself.

'That sounds wonderful, but what sort of job could I get here?' asked Lucy dubiously.

'Easy! The city swarms with tourists, especially in the summer months, and the hotels are full of elderly Americans doing the tour of Europe they've been planning for years, not to mention the young back-packers doing it on the cheap. They get everything from food poisoning and sunstroke to heart failure, and they need English-speaking doctors!

'Lots of the bigger hotels have their own regular doctors on call, and some of the local GPs do a roaring trade out of the visitors!'

Lucy was smiling by now, to Valeria's relief.

'It's true—we've got this gorgeous one on the Lido who's always in demand from the tourists. Think about it, Lucy; it could be just what you need.'

Lucy shrugged off the suggestion, but secretly found it intriguing. The idea of spending a full six months' season in Venice was certainly attractive, but how to set about it and persuade Sir Peter and Lady Philippa Hallcross-Spriggs of the advantages was another matter.

As Aubrey's guests made their way to the restaurant on foot, there being no transport other than by water in Venice, they met groups of laughing musicians and masked dancers—some dressed in medieval costume, others in fantastic outfits with heads of birds and animals.

Dr Gianni Scogliera explained that there was to be a saint's day celebration in St Mark's Square that evening, and just for a moment Lucy thought she saw

Ponti's dark eyes flashing as a knot of merrymakers swirled past them in the dusk of the Mercerie where the lighted shop windows glittered. She had assumed that he would be with Gabriella on the Lido, but surely there he was, with a laughing girl on each arm, gazing up at him adoringly. Could she be mistaken?

A candle-lit table for six awaited the party at the restaurant, decorated with a centrepiece of spring flowers arranged around an ornamental silver nightingale, the emblem which gave L'Usignolo Argento its name.

As Lucy had foreseen, Gianni Scogliera had been tipped off by Aubrey that he was to escort Dr Corsini and the arrangement seemed to suit them both as they chatted happily together. Sir Peter partnered a rather silent Meg Elstone, while Lucy received the undivided attention of Aubrey.

Valeria caught her eye with a significant look which plainly said, What's your problem? Your future's there beside you, ready and waiting! Lucy merely shrugged at her friend, wishing that she felt as sure.

Menus were put before them, together with two bottles of champagne on ice. From the pasta dishes Lucy chose *farfalle*, shaped like little butterflies, with fresh salmon in a cream sauce and accompanied by endive salad and olives.

Laughter rose from the table and Sir Peter beamed upon them all, especially his lovely daughter; as always, heads turned to look at the tall, willowy girl, her figure shown off to perfection in a clinging silk jersey dress of a deep violet colour.

She saw that her father clearly approved of his

private secretary as an ideal match for her, as worthy as any man could be to carry off such a prize as his darling only child.

And she heard Aubrey's whisper close to her ear.

'Perhaps this trip to Venice is meant to show us our destiny, Lucinda.'

She smiled, and while she considered her reply she heard Sir Peter telling Valeria and Gianni about her adventures of the previous evening.

'Rather a dicey moment, I gather, when Lucinda had to give the kiss of life on the deck of the *vaporetto*,' she heard him say, and immediately corrected him.

'No, Daddy, it was Dr Ponti who gave mouth-to-mouth resuscitation after fishing this boy out of the Lagoon.'

'*Ponti*?'

Valeria and Gianni looked at each other and raised their eyebrows.

'Not Pino? *O mio Dio!*' exclaimed Valeria. 'How many girls would envy you such a chance, Lucy. He's the GP I was telling you about earlier—the one who's always in big demand by the tourists!'

'Especially at the Venice Film Festival when the Lido's full of film stars and directors,' added Gianni with a grin. 'Remember that young starlet last year who fainted whenever he came near to her?'

'Oh, so many girls throw themselves at Pino and think they're the love of his life!' said Valeria impatiently.

'Yes, that was why he had to flee to the mainland after the festival—to make his escape from two fiancées,' laughed Gianni.

'Go on, you're only envious,' teased his partner. 'Actually, he's very good with *real* patients, like the ones that go to the Villa Luisa.'

She turned to Lucy, her face more serious. 'You remember me telling you about that place, Lucy— the one owned by the countess? She's a qualified nurse and Pino runs his practice from there, with a consulting-room and a dispensary. It's a bit run-down, but there's a lovely, friendly atmosphere and they've got a superb cook—as good as any in the big hotels.'

'Lucky devil, Pino,' reflected Gianni good-humouredly. 'What with the divine *Contessa* and all the other home comforts of the Villa Luisa, it is no wonder he stays on.'

He chuckled, and Lucy realised that she had not eaten a mouthful during this intriguing exchange. She had also completely forgotten Aubrey's tender senti-ment, and noticed that his mouth had tightened a little. She was ashamed of her neglect of her host, and gave him a vague little smile.

'Are you enjoying the *farfalle*, Lucinda?' he asked.

'Oh, yes, absolutely delicious,' she said quickly.

'Good. I only asked because you were not eating it,' he said, and Lucy picked up her fork to do it justice.

When Aubrey led her out onto the little dance floor and held her in a light embrace, while Sir Peter looked on fondly and Meg Elstone stared down at her untouched plate, Lucy experienced the same awk-wardness as in the gondola. Also, she was feeling a little irritated by Portwood's possessive attitude—he had hardly addressed a word to his other guests.

When Valeria said that she would have to be going, in order to board the midnight *vaporetto* for the Lido, Lucy insisted on seeing her off, so the party broke up soon after eleven.

'Have you thought any more about a temporary job here for the summer?' asked Valeria as they tidied themselves in the ladies' cloakroom.

'I honestly don't know, Val,' sighed Lucy, shaking her head.

'Why don't you think about it? It sounds as if you did a pretty good job last night with that poor boy. You need to get back to being a doctor, my girl!'

Lucy made no reply, but deep in her heart she felt that Valeria Corsini was right.

'Look, I'm off this weekend and I haven't planned anything special—what about you coming over to stay in my flat?' suggested Valeria. 'See what you think of life on the Lido!'

'Oh, Val, are you sure? That sounds just wonderful,' sighed Lucy longingly. 'I'll have to choose my moment to tell Daddy, though.'

'Good! Come over on Friday evening, then,' said her friend firmly. 'I shall be furious if you don't.'

There was an atmosphere of carnival in the city that night, and brightly lit boats sailed down the Grand Canal to the strains of music and singing. Gianni Scogliera held Valeria's arm as they walked towards St Mark's Square, while Aubrey escorted Lucy. Sir Peter had said that he felt tired and had returned to the hotel, accompanied by Meg Elstone, who'd declined to join the two couples.

As the quartet approached the great piazza the

sounds of violins, songs and laughter filled the air, and before the floodlit cathedral a colourful scene greeted them—of musicians in a half-circle and masked dancers leaping and spinning to the music; the women's skirts flared out as the men held them by their waists and tossed them up in the air to shouts of applause.

A man's clear tenor voice rose above the violins, singing an ancient ballad about the swiftly passing joys of youth.

> *'Quant è bella giovinezza*
> *Che si fugge tuttavia!'*

Lucy's spirits rose and her irritation vanished, though Portwood kept a restraining hand on her arm.

'Oh, look over there, Lucy,' said Valeria, pointing to a figure on the edge of the spectators. 'There's one who doesn't waste any of his youth!'

Lucy glanced in the indicated direction, and gave a start as she looked straight into two darkly gleaming eyes beneath sable brows. In the present mood of carnival she could imagine that the fine, lean features might have belonged to a Venetian prince of the Renaissance.

'Guarda li—c'è Giuseppe Ponti!' exclaimed Gianni with a laugh.

Lucy tried to look away from Ponti, but found herself riveted by his hypnotic gaze. So engrossed was she by the unexpected encounter that she failed to notice one of the male dancers break away from the others and silently approach her. He was a big, muscular man with the stealth of a panther, and wore a grotesque mask with a huge bird's beak.

Both Lucy and her escort were taken unawares as the cloaked figure pounced and whirled her off her feet amidst shouts of laughter from the bystanders and a roar of protest from Portwood.

Lucy was completely helpless as her body was lifted up and twirled around the head of the giant who held her in a steely grip, one huge hand in the middle of her back, the other grasping her left hip.

The stars circled madly above her and the lamps of the piazza blurred crazily as she flew round between the man's hands and then descended into his powerful arms. He swung her backwards until her hair nearly touched the paving, and she gave a cry as the menacing beak loomed above her.

She hardly knew what happened next, but there was a shout and a scuffle as other hands took hold of her and a man's voice growled, *'Levati di mezzo!'* The beak hastily withdrew, there was a yelp of pain as a sharp kick landed on a leg and Lucy found herself transferred to another man's arms. Arms that she remembered from the previous evening.

'Pino!' she panted, dishevelled and giddy.

'Va bene, cara Lucia—sei sicura con me,' he was saying, assuring her that she was safe as she clung to him, gradually regaining her breath and balance. The tenor's song was resounding in her ears.

'Che vuol esse lieto sia,
Di doman ne c'è certezza!'

Pino began to translate the words for her in a low, urgent whisper.

'Do you hear, Lucia? He tells us to be happy, be merry, today, tonight—for we may not see tomorrow, no?'

There was an almost irresistible temptation in the deep, accented voice and in his warm breath on her face. Her arms were already round his neck, and when he lowered his dark head her mouth was ready for the touch of his lips—soft at first, then harder and fiercer.

There was a recklessness in his kiss, reflecting the words of the song, but Lucy could not allow herself to forget that she was with friends and in a public place; it cost her a tremendous effort to release herself and draw back to arm's length.

She was immediately grabbed, none too gently, by a spluttering Aubrey Portwood, and Valeria was anxiously asking her if she was all right.

'Lucinda! What the hell are you thinking of?' demanded Aubrey. 'You could have been dropped and seriously injured by that fool of a dancer. And as for that impudent show-off Ponti—how he *dared* to—to—'

He broke off, for the object of his wrath had silently disappeared into the thinning crowd. 'Damned coward can't even face me,' he muttered.

'It's all right, Mr Portwood, all sorts of silly things go on at carnival time,' soothed Valeria tactfully, while Gianni marvelled at Ponti's boldness and wished that he had the nerve to try the same tactics with Valeria.

Lucy was spared having to give any explanations because by this time the *vaporetto* was about to depart, and Valeria had to take her leave of them.

'Thank you for a wonderful meal and all your generosity, Mr Portwood,' she said, politely shaking hands with her grim-faced host, and, turning to Lucy, she gave her an affectionate hug and whispered, 'Don't forget, you're coming to stay for the weekend—give me a ring tomorrow!'

Gianni took the opportunity to kiss Valeria in the Italian way—on each cheek—and as they waved goodbye Lucy thought she saw Ponti among the passengers on the *vaporetto*, but was not certain.

I'm not certain about anything at all, she thought to herself as she and Aubrey walked back to the hotel in silence. He had no words to voice his fury, and was disappointed in Lucinda for offering no resistance to that confounded Italian doctor who had shown him up by rescuing her.

And Lucy had no words to describe how she felt about her rescuer, and the intoxicating pressure of his lips upon hers.

For she had sensed a helpless rage beneath his abandoned behaviour, something almost approaching despair.

And then she thought of the lovely Gabriella.

CHAPTER FOUR

THE chairman was introducing the next speaker.

'And to present Sir Peter's paper on Geographical Distribution of Cardiovascular Disorder in the United Kingdom here is his daughter and research assistant, the Honourable Dr Lucinda Hallcross-Spriggs.'

The Thursday afternoon session of the Venice convention was the highspot for the junior Minister, who proudly watched the slim figure in a blue suit and crisp white blouse ascend the podium. Beside him his private secretary sat smiling a little tensely; Aubrey was still feeling shaken by the scene in the Piazza San Marco, and Lucinda's unaccountable behaviour.

Lucy hid her own emotions under a cool exterior, though her eyes swept the assembly to see if Ponti was present; thankfully there was no sign of him, and she began confidently.

'A survey of this kind must inevitably involve a study of population levels, social grading and employment—or unemployment—in any given area,' she said, her clear voice ringing through the hall. 'We decided to divide the United Kingdom into five regions. May I have the first slide, please?'

The curtains were drawn and the projector switched on, throwing a highly magnified diagram onto a white screen. Picking up a pointer, Lucy outlined boundaries and indicated major towns. With the hall darkened, she could no longer see her audience.

'Let us look at areas of heavy industry, concentrated in the north, both east and west—also parts of Scotland and the Midlands,' she continued. 'Next slide, please.'

The first twenty minutes passed, and Lucy talked endlessly of numbers—of GP referrals, outpatient attendances and hospital admissions; mortality rates were adjusted to show percentages of age groups and gender differences. She was thankful for a silently attentive audience; there was none of the murmuring and fidgeting that had accompanied some of the lectures.

'Now let us look at the incidence of respiratory disorders,' she went on. 'There is a close correlation with cardiac disease, and the statistics show some surprising facts.'

Forty minutes passed, and Lucy took a drink of water from the glass on the table. It was tepid. She longed to take off her jacket but felt that it would be unprofessional, even though some of the delegates were sitting in their shirt-sleeves. She glanced at her wristwatch—it was time to sum up.

'In the light of the evidence Sir Peter and I have brought together, several important conclusions emerge,' she said, raising her voice a little and putting down the pointer. As she ended her lecture she completely forgot to ask for the curtains to be opened, and her final words were uttered in darkness.

Complete silence followed, and Lucy realised her mistake with dismay.

'Oh, please could we have the projector switched off and the curtains drawn back?' she asked hastily.

There was a stir in the middle of the hall, and a male voice sharply barked, *'Svegliatevi!'*—wake up! The projector clicked off and sunlight flooded in on the delegates who straightened themselves in their seats and tried to look alert, though one elderly man was snoring until prodded in the ribs. His loud *'E' finito?'* caused a brief ripple of laughter, hastily suppressed.

Lucy stood before them, gradually registering the fact that she had failed to breathe life into the statistics she had so carefully checked over with her father, though he and Aubrey were smiling at her—but was that a gleam of amusement in Meg Elstone's eyes? Lucy swallowed. Heavens above, she thought, it must have been the dullest, most uninspiring lecture of the week. . .

And that wasn't all. There, in the middle of the hall, sat Pino Ponti, apparently none the worse for his exertions of the previous evening. She felt her face flushing crimson, and could not meet his eyes.

'Are there any questions for Dr Hallcross-Spriggs?' asked the chairman.

There was dead silence, and the chairman was about to conclude with his routine thanks when a hand went up.

'Ah, I see that Dr Ponti has a question. Please speak into the microphone, *dottore*.'

Lucy's whole body went rigid. Was he about to humiliate her by asking her something she could not answer? Oh, let me be able to give immediate, accurate information! she silently prayed.

Taking the proffered microphone, Ponti began, *'Dottoressa*, I am impressed by the extensive research

you and your father have done.' He looked towards
Sir Peter and received a contemptuous glare from
Portwood. 'Yet there is something I cannot reconcile
with what I know of you, *dottoressa*, and it is a
personal question I have for you.'

Lucy drew a deep breath and forced herself to meet
those probing dark eyes.

'Go ahead, *dottore*,' she said with cool formality.
'I am prepared to answer any reasonable question on
Sir Peter's paper. Only may I request that you come
to the point?'

Everybody in the hall was now listening intently
to this spirited exchange.

'*Con piacere*. My question is this: how can you,
as a doctor, fail to be moved by the human suffering
behind these columns of numbers? Did you and your
father go to see these places of poverty, of unemployment, of stress, of poor nutrition—all the factors that
lead to cardiac failure? Did you never long to see the
faces behind the figures, Dr Hallcross-Spriggs?'

Lucy hoped that her trembling knees did not show
beneath the narrow skirt that only just covered them.
He's getting at me, she thought, showing me up in
front of the convention. When Ponti sat down, all
eyes were upon her to see how she would react to
his challenge. There was a brief pause before she
replied, speaking slowly and deliberately.

'Thank you for your question, Dr Ponti. You have
raised an important issue. Statistics are not easy to
put over, not being dramatic material. They have not
the same appeal as case histories.'

'Of course not!' Sir Peter's angry retort cut in,
but Lucy held up a warning finger to her father

not to interrupt and continued calmly.

'In compiling this research, Sir Peter and I found that we had actually to block out any emotive reaction as being unhelpful to our work, which has to be precise and factual.

'These dry-as-dust figures will be of great value in deciding where cardiac units should be built, where health centres should be especially aware of early signs and preventive measures—where money should be spent, in fact. These statistics will eventually find their way into health campaigns, television programmes, posters, newspapers and magazines, targeted to areas and groups most at risk.'

She was encouraged by the stirrings of agreement in the hall, and allowed herself to send one of her radiant smiles in Ponti's direction.

'The world of medicine has many aspects,' she went on. 'One doctor may dedicate his life to serving as a medical missionary in a remote part of the third world. Another may spend his or her time in libraries and record offices, as I do. Yet another may find there are rich pickings to be made out of the tourist trade, *dottore*.'

She paused again to savour the smiles and significant glances her words had provoked, and saw that Ponti's expression had gone blank at hearing the unmistakable dig; she mentally awarded herself a point.

'Our profession is nothing if not diverse, and all kinds of abilities are needed. Now, are there any further questions?'

An enthusiastic round of applause accompanied Lucy as she stepped down from the podium and made her way back to her seat beside her father.

'Wonderful, darling, I'm so proud of you!' he beamed, standing up and kissing her flushed cheek, while Aubrey positively glowed his satisfaction. He dismissed Lucy's untypical behaviour in St Mark's Square as a temporary aberration. She was entirely reinstated in his eyes, and he only just managed to restrain himself from kissing her too.

'Well done, Lucinda, you well and truly thrashed him, and God knows he deserved it.'

Lucy was ready to faint with relief. Far from humiliating her in public, Ponti had done her a favour and had turned her uninspiring lecture into a personal triumph—a fitting return for the way he had turned her life upside down in the past forty-eight hours.

That evening Lucy told her father of her intention to stay over the weekend at Valeria's flat on the Lido.

'It's such a heaven-sent opportunity to see something of the place while I'm here, Daddy,' she said persuasively, though she was a little taken aback by his reaction, for he clearly had no intention of leaving her behind.

'What a marvellous idea, darling! I'll get Aubrey to cancel our flights and find somewhere to stay on the Lido,' he said happily, quite unaware of her dismayed expression.

'They say the Excelsior's a good place,' Sir Peter enthused over dinner, but Aubrey steered the jovial baronet towards a smaller hotel near to a golf course.

'I'll take you through a few rounds, Aubrey—good exercise, and a chance to get to know each other on a more personal footing,' smiled Sir Peter with a meaningful look in Lucy's direction. The booking was duly made, and it was arranged that the two men should transfer to the Hotel des Deux Lions on Friday evening when the convention ended. Meg Elstone declined to accompany them, however.

'Thank you, but I shall return to Gatwick. I have plans for the weekend,' she said briefly.

'Really? Well, I don't want your arrangements to be upset, Meg,' said Sir Peter, a little dashed by her curt manner.

'Neither would I, after a week of sitting and listening to some of the stuff I've had to endure,' muttered the typist, half under her breath. 'Excuse me, please, I'm not staying for dessert or coffee.'

'I just wish I knew what's bugging Meg,' said Lucy as the girl walked briskly away without a backward glance. 'I've done my best to include her in everything, but she's so prickly. Do you think it's boyfriend trouble? I don't like to ask her outright, in case she tells me to mind my own business.'

'Could be just jealousy,' smiled Aubrey. 'With a girl like you around, there's not much chance for a prim little thing like Miss Elstone!'

'But if she's got a real problem, I ought to be doing something about it,' persisted Lucy worriedly.

'Oh, never mind her, Lucinda, just think of the weekend ahead! A most inviting prospect, don't you think?'

Lucy did not reply, for she had decided to spend as much time as possible with Valeria. More than ever she needed breathing-space to sort herself out— to consider her renewed interest in putting her doctor's degree into clinical practice.

All set to enjoy herself, Lucy had no idea of the wider horizons about to open up for her, changing her way of life and presenting her with a new set of values.

Waking up in Valeria's pretty apartment on Saturday morning, Lucy stretched luxuriously as her hostess sailed in with a tray of coffee and warm croissants with butter.

'Another glorious day, Lucy—do you fancy riding? There are some stables, where I hire a lovely little brown mare,' suggested Valeria as she poured out the coffee.

'I haven't brought any togs,' replied Lucy doubtfully.

'You've got trousers that will do, and I can lend you a hat,' said Valeria. 'The only thing is, Lucy, I'll have to leave you for about an hour at some point. There's this antenatal patient I ought to call on. She's been resting in the hospital, and I've let her out on condition that I can check on her to see that she's behaving herself.'

'Even on your weekend off?' asked Lucy in some surprise. 'Can't a midwife call?'

'I feel specially responsible for Maria Capogna. She's got a heart murmur, and also happens to be the sister of Pino Ponti,' explained Valeria. 'She's on the staff of the Villa Luisa, that place I was telling you about.'

Lucy was at once all attention. 'His *sister*?' She had not thought of Pino as having family close at hand.

'Yes, she's the assistant cook and her husband's

the gardener and odd-job man—a nice, ordinary couple expecting their first child. On Maria's very first visit to the antenatal clinic I picked up this dodgy valve, and when we did an ECG there was a noticeable irregularity on the P wave, due to atrial hypertrophy.

'It turned out she'd had rheumatic fever as a child and you know how it can leave children with valve lesions, though she'd been symptom-free. The extra strain of pregnancy is beginning to take its toll at thirty weeks.'

Lucy's eyes widened, and she set aside her breakfast, clasping her hands around her knees.

'*That* explains why Pino gave such a vivid description of a primigravida with mitral stenosis,' she exclaimed. 'It *was* real to him—his own sister!'

'Yes, I'd heard that Mr d'Arc included her case history in his paper at the convention,' Valeria affirmed.

'And how is she coping now?' asked Lucy, finding herself consumed with interest in this young mother-to-be whom she had never met.

'Reasonably well, except that she gets a bit short of breath. The least bit of exertion and she starts to pant, bless her.'

'Any cyanosis?' inquired Lucy, with instinctive curiosity as a doctor.

'Not as yet, and no angina pain or haemoptysis, heaven forbid!'

'And after delivery?' persisted Lucy.

'Difficult to say. Mr d'Arc says he'll review her at six weeks postnatal and then at three months to consider a mitral valvotomy. There's bound to be more babies, and— Lucy, you've gone quite pale! Is anything the matter?'

Lucy had been gazing out of the window at the sea. She now turned and looked at Valeria, her violet-blue eyes alight with concern.

'Let me come with you, Val. I want to see this patient I've heard so much about.'

'Of course, if you want to. I'll tell the *contessa* you're a visiting doctor friend of mine.'

Which is what I am, thought Lucy, a visiting doctor. Would Pino be there? After their last encounter, she could surely face him on an equal footing!

The Villa Luisa stood back from a tree-lined avenue behind wrought-iron gates, guarded by stone lions on each side. From Lucy's very first sight of the house— with its solid stonework, topped by a shallow, sloping, red-tiled roof, its arched casement windows and wide, balustraded balconies—she was drawn to it as to a welcoming haven.

There was something reassuring about its graceful lines and, although the wooden shutters needed a coat of paint and the carved stone frames were somewhat weathered, the general aspect was of a gracious mansion, lived in and loved. It stood within a semi-circle of tall trees and evergreens, with a well-kept garden of shrubs, a daisied lawn and a little pond with a smiling stone nymph at its centre; it was entirely charming.

Valeria went ahead, mounting the steps to the porch and pushing on the half-opened panelled door.

'*Buongiorno! Siamo le dottoresse!*' she called.

'*Dr Valeria, benvenuta!*' replied a woman's

pleasantly deep, cultured voice, and a tall, elegant lady of about forty-five approached. She wore an apron over a long skirt and greeted Valeria warmly, raising a questioning eye towards Lucy.

'Contessa, this is Dr Lucy Spriggs, who has been attending the Venice convention this week,' said Valeria. 'Lucy, meet the Contessa Cecilia Favaro, *padrona* of the Villa Luisa.'

Lucy took the cool hand held out to her with formal politeness.

'*Molto lieto, contessa,*' she murmured.

The lady informed Valeria that Signora Capogna was resting with another newly arrived patient, and asked them to follow her. They went through a rather cluttered sitting-room, with an ornate marble fireplace and a piano piled high with music scores, into a hallway lit by a stained-glass window.

The *contessa* ushered them into a small lift whose gilded gates clanked shut and opened again on the second floor, where she led them along a passage lined with framed paintings and onto a north-facing balcony.

Lucy got an immediate impression of wicker furniture with faded cushions, trailing scarlet blooms in urns and hanging-baskets, and three playful kittens who seemed to be everywhere; in one of two large wicker chairs sat a plump, round-faced, pregnant woman, and in the other was Gabriella Rasi.

'Lucia!' There was no mistaking the pleasure in the actress's face and voice as she held out both hands; Lucy again experienced a sense of instant rapport, and went to her at once.

'Come and talk while Maria goes for her antenatal

check-up,' said Gabriella. 'How long can you stay?'

Lucy glanced towards the *contessa*, aware that those observant eyes were missing nothing, though she appeared to be busy with her pot plants—pulling out dead leaves and checking the moisture of the soil. Lucy sat down beside Gabriella, who was stroking a little black, white and ginger cat on her lap.

'Meet Briciola, the mother of these naughty *micini*! Oh, it's so restful here I feel better already,' the girl confided, fondling the cat's ears. 'Cecilia spoils me disgracefully, and encourages me to be lazy—the place has cast a spell over me!'

Lucy could quite understand. The balcony gave a magnificent view of the Lido, looking towards the northern shore and Venice drowsing across the Lagoon beneath an arching blue sky.

'Lucia, I'm so worried about Maria's weak heart,' Gabriella went on, lowering her voice and resting her delicate hand on Lucy's shoulder. 'She *will* insist on waiting on me when she should be resting. Her baby's due in another couple of months, and I'm so sorry for poor Silvio, her husband—that's him down there in the garden with the wheelbarrow, see—he must be so troubled about her. It is very sad, yes?'

Lucy smiled. 'You must not worry about her, *cara mia*, she is very well cared for,' she said gently, thinking how frail this girl looked in comparison to the rosy, well-rounded Maria—who now reappeared, all smiles, while Valeria put her stethoscope back into her leather bag, together with the sphygmomanometer for measuring blood pressure.

The *contessa* rejoined the group. 'Good, now we are ready for coffee,' she said. '*No*, Maria, sit down and put your feet up on the stool. *I* shall fetch the tray.'

Maria smiled and shrugged as she lowered her ample form into the wicker chair.

'Nobody argues with the *contessa*!' she said in Italian, and Lucy noted her snub nose and dark button eyes; she had a good-humoured peasant's face, not at all like Pino's—though her jet-black eyebrows were the same shape as his.

'You will take coffee, *dottoressa*?' asked the *contessa*, and Lucy felt the change in her manner, no longer aloof and formal.

'Thank you, *contessa*, that's most kind.' She took the cup and shortbread biscuit offered.

'Do you plan to stay long on the Lido, *dottoressa*?'

'No, Daddy and I—Sir Peter and I are leaving on Tuesday, *contessa*.'

'Please call me Cecilia.'

'Thank you—and please call me Lucia!'

Why had she said the Italian version of her name? It had slipped out naturally, before she had stopped to think.

'You have work in England, Lucia?'

'Yes, in—er—my father's ministry, actually,' replied Lucy, faltering a little. 'I'm a statistician.'

'You mean you do not work with sick people?'

'No, not at present—but I shall return to practical work soon,' Lucy heard herself saying with conviction. 'Yes, Cecilia, I shall practise as a doctor again before long.'

'We shall have need of help here at the Villa Luisa if you know of anybody interested,' said Cecilia seriously. 'Dr Ponti has a large practice, and gets called out to hotels at all hours. We take patients who are receiving *radioterapia* at the Ospedale Civile in Venice, and some of them need a lot of care. I have three good nurses, but would like another doctor on call.'

Lucy's heart leapt at hearing this, but she gave no sign of interest. 'I suppose that you will have Signora Capogna to care for until her delivery,' she remarked casually.

'Yes, indeed, and poor Signorina Rasi will need all the love and support we can give her,' continued Cecilia, lowering her voice. 'Dr Ponti fears the worst. We are waiting for the laboratory results on Monday, and he will have to tell—'

'Look, my brother's car has just turned in at the gate!' cried Maria, waving from the balcony.

Cecilia went down to greet Ponti and presumably have a private word with him before he saw the visitors. Lucy braced herself to face Pino again, and began to collect up the coffee-cups.

'We'd better be going, hadn't we?' she said to Valeria.

'Oh, stay a little longer,' begged Gabriella. 'See, Briciola has taken much liking to you!'

Lucy smiled and yielded, sitting down beside the actress and asking her about her career.

'I am due to start filming in Rome, but this silly anaemia is causing much delay,' Gabriella sighed. 'For so long I thought it was just laziness, yet I love my work and have twice put off marriage to the man I adore because of it. Do you think I am very foolish?'

'How can Lucia answer that?' enquired a deep voice behind Lucy, and she felt Pino's hand on her shoulder briefly. He went to kiss Gabriella, and then sat down beside his sister.

'So, what says Dr Corsini of Maria?' he inquired, smiling. 'Has she been a good girl?'

'Very good,' reported Valeria. 'Blood pressure normal, foetal heart fine, mamma's heart coping well.'

'*Eccellente!* So no problems to report to our renowned obstetrician who is coming from Paris this weekend!'

At hearing this, Gabriella clasped her hands together eagerly.

'Pino! Is Findlay coming here? Today?'

'*Si, cara mia, oggi o domani*—perhaps this evening, perhaps tomorrow, depending on when he can get away.'

Lucy heard the tenderness in his voice, but a certain hardness in the set of his jaw indicated that he was under a fair amount of pressure.

'Do you hear that, Lucia?' breathed Gabriella, turning shining eyes towards her. 'My darling Findlay is coming all the way from Paris to see Maria. He is doing a case history on her, so you will meet him!'

Lucy was bewildered. 'Is this Mr Findlay d'Arc, the specialist whose paper you presented?' she asked, glancing towards Pino.

'One and the same,' he nodded. 'He was senior registrar when I was a mere houseman doing my obstetrics at Padua, where we met each other and Gabriella who was filming near her home. All the men were in love with her, but d'Arc was the lucky one.'

'Oh, don't tell such stories, Pino!' protested Gabriella, laughing.

'It's the truth, I tell you! I challenged him to fight a duel, but—'

'What nonsense you talk, Pino! Do not listen to him, Lucia; he and Findlay are the best of friends,' smiled Gabriella, overjoyed at the thought of seeing her lover again so soon. 'Oh, must you leave already?'

Lucy had risen, seeing that Valeria was also preparing to go.

'Yes, you must excuse us now, Gabriella, but I will come back to see you before I leave for England,' she promised and, leaning towards the girl, she kissed her pale cheek and laid a reassuring hand on her shoulder.

Cecilia Favaro noted the leave-taking, and added a word as she saw the two young women out.

'You will always be welcome here while Gabriella is in my care, Lucia, because I see that you are good for her,' she said simply, and their eyes met in mutual understanding.

Lucy's thoughts were in a whirl as she left the villa. Even if Pino had been in love with Gabriella, she reasoned—even if he were still in love with her, the girl herself clearly had a long-standing relationship with this specialist, d'Arc, who was coming over from Paris ostensibly to see Pino's sister. It sounded as if Pino had sent for him as a matter of urgency, so that he would be with Gabriella when the test results were known.

In sharing the suspense that hung over the Villa Luisa this weekend, Lucy hardly dared to try to analyse her own feelings in this complex network of relationships.

Saturday and Sunday passed in sunny walks, rides and picnics, while Sir Peter and Aubrey improved their golf handicaps in friendly competition. There were convivial dinners at the Hotel des Deux Lions when Lucy and Valeria joined the two men. Sir Peter visibly relaxed after the convention, but although Lucy did her best to match his mood her thoughts never strayed far from the Villa Luisa.

On the Sunday morning she rose early and attended Mass at the beautiful little chapel in the grounds of the Ospedale Al Mare. Afterwards she lingered for a while, thankful for the peace and tranquillity of the place.

'You are a visitor here, *signorina*?' asked a pleasant male voice in Italian, and Lucy turned to see the *cappellano*, or chaplain, standing close by. He was dressed in the plain brown habit of a Franciscan, and his kind, sensitive face inspired instant trust.

'Padre Renato.' He held out his hand in a welcoming gesture. 'I always notice a new face.'

'Lucy Spriggs—*Dottoressa Lucia*,' she smiled, and introduced herself as a friend of Dr Corsini. He at once nodded in recognition, and clearly knew all the staff by name. Lucy enquired whether he visited outside the hospital, and soon discovered that he was a friend of the *contessa* and visited the Villa Luisa regularly.

'Oh, Padre, could you go there tomorrow afternoon?' begged Lucy eagerly. 'I think that the *contessa* would be very pleased to see you.'

He nodded understandingly.

'*Va bene, dottoressa.* I shall remember to return a book to the *contessa* that I have borrowed for too long, yes?'

Lucy could have hugged him, but made do with shaking his hand and thanking him from her heart. It was good to know that this wise and gentle man would be there to comfort her friends if the news was not good.

Valeria was back on duty on Monday morning at eight, so Lucy went out walking alone; her feet seemed to have a mind of their own, for they took her straight to the house which constantly occupied her thoughts.

As soon as she turned in at the gates she was conscious of an invisible cloud casting its shadow over the villa and its occupants, and as she approached the half-open front door she heard ominous murmurs. A man's protesting voice sounded harsh with emotion, and the *contessa* was speaking rapidly in a low tone.

Lucy braced her shoulders and pushed the door open, stepping into the cool sitting-room. Three faces turned to look at her—Cecilia, Pino and another man, tall and aesthetic in appearance. His face was flushed and all three seemed agitated, though the *contessa* managed a smile when she saw Lucy.

'*Dottoressa Lucia, grazie al Signore!*' she sighed in relief. 'Perhaps you can bring some English calm and common sense to this house!'

Pino looked apologetically at Lucy, while the other

man turned away impatiently and leaned his arms on the top of the piano. Cecilia went to his side and put a hand on his shoulder, but when she tried to speak to him he turned his head away from her.

'Findlay, please—' she remonstrated but, shaking off her hand, he strode out of the front door without a word.

Pino came to Lucy's side and took her hand in his; his dark eyes were deeply troubled, and Lucy knew without a word being said that they had heard the results of the tests.

'Tell me,' she said steadily.

'The worst, Lucia.' His voice was barely audible, and she clasped his hand in both of her own.

'Go on,' she prompted.

'Acute lymphoblastic leukaemia,' he answered. 'Raised white cell count with many immature leucocytes. Low platelet count.'

'I see.' It was like hearing a sentence passed. 'What does the professor of oncology propose to do?'

'Have her in straight away for immediate blood transfusion and review. Start chemotherapy, if indicated.' He inclined his head in the direction the other man had taken. 'Findlay says he won't let her go, and wants her to see a specialist in Paris—but he'll have to face facts. She must not be subjected to any more trauma than is absolutely necessary.'

'When did Mr d'Arc arrive?' she asked.

'Yesterday,' muttered Pino. 'I could see he was shocked when he saw her, but he can't—or won't—believe the implications of what the lab phoned through to us this morning.'

'You can understand how he feels, Pino.'

'Yes, but he's no bloody use to Gabriella like this. The rest of us have all had to hide our feelings, for God's sake!'

'Shh! Anger is no good to her either,' Lucy said quickly. 'Who's with her now?'

'One of the nurses and my sister.'

'Right, I'll have a word with her,' said Lucy at once. 'May I go up, Cecilia?'

'Of course, Lucia, *cara mia*. She is on the balcony.'

'I'll come with you,' began Pino, but Lucy held up her hand with a new air of authority.

'No, Pino, I need to see her alone.'

With a firm sense of purpose she made her way up to the second-floor balcony, where she found Gabriella lying on a divan with Briciola and her kittens. A subdued Maria Capogna sat at her side, and a nurse was rearranging her pillows.

'Lucia! Oh, how it pleases me to see you!' she sighed, holding out her arms. 'Everybody is so full of—of *miseria* this morning, just because I have to go into hospital and have a blood transfusion. *I* do not mind, so why should Findlay be so cross about it? If it makes me well again and gives me back my energy—oh, Lucia, *cara*, please tell Findlay and Pino to accept what the good *professore* says, and to smile for my sake!'

There were tears of bewilderment lurking in her soft blue eyes, and Lucy knew that she had to hide her own emotion at all costs. She smiled at both Gabriella and Maria.

'*I* don't know—these men!' she said with mock exasperation, sitting down on the divan and putting her arms around the slight figure. 'Leave it to me,

Gabriella, and I'll explain exactly how you feel. I'll make them understand, you'll see.'

'Ah, I knew I could rely on you, Lucia—didn't I say so, Maria?' said Gabriella triumphantly. 'I feel better already with you here. You're so strong, Lucia. And you won't leave me now, will you? *Non lasciarmi!*'

With the girl's head resting on her shoulder, Lucy hesitated. She saw Cecilia Favaro come on to the balcony and take a seat beside Maria. The nurse lingered, waiting like the others for Lucy's reply to Gabriella's plea.

When Lucy spoke, it was with calm deliberation. 'No, Gabriella, *cara*, I will not leave you. I will stay here at the Villa Luisa as a doctor, and do everything I can to help look after the contessa's guests.'

She saw the look of thankfulness that transformed Cecilia's face, and heard her muttered '*Grazie alla Madre di Dio.*'

But how was she going to tell her father that the Villa Luisa had a new resident medical officer—herself?

CHAPTER FIVE

As soon as Gabriella had fallen into a relaxed and peaceful doze, Cecilia beckoned Lucy to her chaotic little office.

'There is much to be done, *cara Lucia*,' she said eagerly. 'First we must contact the British Consulate in Venice to get for you a temporary work permit. It is fortunate that I have friends in the Department of Health, and can cut through much official—er—red tape, yes?'

Lucy's head whirled as her mind began to grasp the impact of what she had done. 'My documents are with my luggage in Valeria's apartment—I'll have to ring her—' she began.

'And we must ring the airport to cancel your flight tomorrow. Do it now, before you change your mind,' advised the *contessa*, handing her the telephone. 'As for the luggage, no problem—Giuseppino can fetch it when he returns from his calls.'

She spoke airily, but the mention of Pino's name was a reminder to Lucy that she and he would be living under the same roof, and there could be some overlapping of their work with the patients staying at the Villa Luisa.

How would he react to this unexpected appointment? Would he, heaven forbid, think that she was chasing him, as so many other women apparently did?

If so, she would quickly let him see his mistake: she had been engaged by the *contessa*, who urgently needed another resident doctor, and Lucy had seized a heaven-sent opportunity to return to medical practice, caring for the kind of seriously ill patients that the Villa Luisa served. The fact that Dr Ponti ran his surgery from here had nothing to do with it. . .

'We have not talked of money, Lucia.' Cecilia's voice broke in on these reflections. 'I hope you realise that I cannot pay as much as you would earn if employed by the Department of Health.' She then named a figure well below Lucy's salary at the Ministry.

'That will be fine, Cecilia, honestly—I can't wait to begin proper work again. Just think, if I hadn't met Gabriella—'

'Ah, yes, dear Gabriella.' Cecilia's face was grave. 'Let us hope that Findlay will calm himself soon and face the truth.'

Lucy now felt free to ask about the relationship between the actress and the eminent specialist, and the *contessa* was quite willing to talk to her new staff member.

'Many men have been in love with Gabriella— actors, directors and others—but she has always been a butterfly, refusing to be tied down,' she confided. 'She says her acting comes first, though Findlay d'Arc has always stayed there in the background— he has an apartment in Paris, she has one in Rome— and they have had an—er—arrangement over the years. But now—'

Cecilia raised her shoulders and sighed heavily.

'Heaven knows what will happen. Her acting career is over, that is sure.'

'And—er—Dr Ponti?' asked Lucy, wondering where the enigmatic Venetian doctor fitted into this scenario.

'Giuseppino? Ah, he knew a long time ago that she was not for him, and he is not a man to take second place in any woman's life, not even Gabriella's!' Cecilia replied with a smile. 'But, although he has had many girlfriends, he has never found one to take her place. He has a—a *reputazione*, yes?' She shrugged. '*Allora, cara mia*, I am grateful that you are here to help us through a difficult time ahead. I pray you may have no regrets.'

Lucy was sure that she never would, but there still remained the hurdle of telling her father, and she lost no time in putting through a call to the Hotel des Deux Lions. When she was told that Sir Peter was on the golf course she left a message for him to phone her back, and then went to be introduced to the three women and one man currently staying at the Villa Luisa, in addition to Gabriella and Maria Capogna.

'I refer to them as my guests, not as patients,' explained Cecilia. 'They occupy single or double rooms, all with balconies—except for the Capognas, who sleep together in an attic room. It is not good that Silvio should be apart from his wife at such a time, no?'

'How are the pa—the guests transported across the Lagoon for their radiotherapy sessions at the Ospedale Civile?' asked Lucy.

'Ah, we have a little inlet from the sea which comes right up to a private landing-stage at the back of the villa,' said Cecilia. 'The ambulances come over to fetch them, and carry them straight to the side entrance of the hospital—you could say they travel door to door by water!'

Lucy remembered seeing the efficient, well-equipped motor-boat *ambulanze* that carried patients swiftly along the canals of Venice, and remarked that Gabriella would soon be making that journey across the Lagoon to be admitted under the professor's care.

'She will go tomorrow morning,' said Cecilia. 'That will give her another evening here with Findlay, so I hope he will make an effort to smile for her.'

Lucy's heart sank. She had promised Gabriella that she would speak to d'Arc, and she still had to face her father. And Pino.

When Sir Peter returned her call at lunchtime, she asked him to come over and see her at the Villa Luisa; if he saw the place for himself and met the *contessa*, she reasoned, he would be more likely to accept her decision.

'And please come alone, Daddy,' she begged. 'I really would prefer to speak with you in private.'

'My dear Lucinda, what on earth are you hatching up?' he asked in his usual jovial tone.

'I'll tell you all about it when I see you, Daddy,' she said, trying to sound reassuring. 'The villa's only fifteen minutes from your hotel.'

'I'll be over straight away after lunch, darling.'

Before he arrived the two doctors returned together, Ponti from his visits to patients and d'Arc from a long, solitary walk along the south shore. Ponti had given his friend a lift up from the Lungomare, and as soon as d'Arc entered the villa he made for the stairs to see Gabriella.

'Not just now, Findlay, she is resting and must not be disturbed,' said the *contessa* firmly. 'You will be able to spend this evening with her.'

D'Arc slumped into an armchair and let his head fall between his hands in a gesture of utter dejection. Pino shrugged at Lucy, who remembered her promise to Gabriella and decided that now was as good a time as any for her to speak.

'Will you introduce me, please?' she asked Pino in her best hostess manner. He raised his eyebrows, but did as requested.

'Oh, by the way, Lucia, this is my friend Findlay d'Arc, graduate of Edinburgh University and citizen of every European capital,' he said with an attempt at lightness. 'Findlay, meet Lucia Spriggs, who is visiting us from England. She met Gabriella while attending the *conferenza*.'

D'Arc raised his head and looked blankly at Lucy, who held out her hand.

'*Molto lieto*—I am very pleased to meet you, Mr d'Arc,' she said pleasantly. 'Gabriella has spoken of you to me.'

His expression lightened a fraction. 'Ah, yes, I remember hearing her speak of you, Lucia—in fact, she has become very attached to you in a short time,' he replied in perfect English, clearly making an effort to be polite.

'As I am to her, Mr d'Arc,' returned Lucy quietly. 'And I am very anxious that she stays happy and calm. The best thing that any of us can do for her now is—well, just to *be there* for her, letting her know that she's loved and supported. It's all that she asks of us—and you.'

He stared at her and frowned slightly; she was also conscious of the look of amazement on Ponti's face at her effrontery.

D'Arc shook his head in a despairing gesture. 'I know that what you say is true, of course, Lucia, but—it's this feeling of helplessness that I can't get round. If there was only something that I could do for her, something positive—'

There was a moment of silence, and then Lucy heard herself speak again.

'Why don't you marry her?'

The effect was electrifying. Cecilia gasped and stood stock-still, while Ponti's jaw dropped open, literally. He seemed unable to believe what he had just heard.

But, after an initial gape of complete surprise, Findlay d'Arc's eyes lit up as if he had suddenly seen a light break in on darkness. Galvanised into action, he rose to his feet and seized Lucy's hand.

'My God, Lucia, you're right, of course— absolutely right! But how did you *know*?'

She was spared the embarrassment of having to say anything more, for at that moment a nurse appeared to say that Signorina Rasi had heard the men's voices and was asking to see Signore d'Arc. He immediately left them to go to her, at which point Pino Ponti turned to Lucy in mixed astonishment and admiration.

'*Bravissima!* Well said, Lucia; you are just what we need here. If only it were possible for you to stay longer!'

Lucy caught Cecilia's eye; the *contessa* looked at Ponti and beamed as she made her announcement.

'I have therefore good news for you, Giuseppino. *La dottoressa* has consented to accept the position of resident medical officer here for the next six months.'

Lucy held her breath while she waited for his reaction. His eyes widened as he clapped a dramatic hand to his forehead.

'*O mio Dio!* How many more shocks have I to take in one day? My heart will not survive, no?'

'Do not be silly, Giuseppino—and pay no attention to him, Lucia. We are extremely grateful to you,' affirmed the contessa.

'*Certamente!* Only—may I be permitted to ask one question, Lucia?'

She met his eyes levelly. 'Go ahead, *dottore*.'

'Tell me, why did you take on this job? What is there in it for the daughter of Sir Peter Hallcross-Spriggs?'

Lucy answered at once in her clearest, most upper-class English accent.

'Perhaps after dealing with all those boring statistics, *dottore*, I feel the need to work with real people again.'

'*Allora!* But if this means—er—*associazone* with me, *dottoressa*—in partnership—how will that please you?'

He was smiling, but there was a real challenge in his tone and a glint in his eyes that put Lucy on her guard. Secretly, the prospect of working in partnership with this man was both inviting and exciting, but it would not do to appear eager. A little imp of mischief sparkled in the violet-blue eyes as she gave her offhand reply.

'Even the best jobs have their disadvantages, Dr Ponti, but I think I shall be able to survive.'

As he stared back at her and the *contessa* laughed aloud, Lucy's attention was diverted by the sight of a bulky figure coming up the steps to the front door.

'Excuse me, please,' she said hastily. 'I have to talk with my father.'

Sir Peter was devastated. He sat upright in the wicker chair that Lucy had placed for him on the back veranda, where the *contessa* had assured her they could talk undisturbed.

'I simply don't believe that I'm hearing this, Lucinda.'

'Daddy, please try to understand—'

'I thought you were happy,' he said miserably. 'You've been much brighter and more confident than at any time since that wretched business at Beltonshaw. Oh, darling, your mother and I couldn't bear to see you get into a state like that again!'

'Daddy, it won't *be* like that again—this is completely different from Beltonshaw.'

She got up and put an arm around his shoulders. A tray of tea and biscuits had been placed on a small table in front of them, but he waved away the cup that Lucy offered and lit a cigar.

'God knows how I'm going to break this to your mother. And there's Aubrey, of course—he'll be terribly upset, poor chap. He thinks the world of you, Lucinda; in fact, your mother and I have both hoped that—'

'Yes, Daddy, I know.' She patted his shoulder affectionately. 'But I'm not so sure that marriage to Aubrey would be right for either of us. I'm a *doctor*, and I want to practise again. I know I found things difficult at Beltonshaw, but there's something here at the Villa Luisa that really draws me. There's this beautiful girl who's dying of a serious bone-marrow disease, and I *know* that I must stay here for her.

'And I could do useful work with other seriously ill patients in a place like this. It's a hospice, rather than a hospital—'

'But there are hospices in England, darling, if you really think you could cope with that sort of work,' said her father, drawing on his cigar and frowning.

'Daddy, dear, I just have to get away from—from home,' she said gently, not wanting to hurt him more than was necessary. 'This is the place where I'm meant to be. I just know it.'

'But you can't just start practising as a doctor in another country, Lucinda! There are all sorts of official details to be sorted out—references, tax, all kinds of stuff.'

'It's not so difficult in another EEC country, Daddy, and the *contessa* is arranging for me to have visitor's status for six months, and practise as a doctor in a private capacity under her sponsorship.'

'This—er—countess, is she a doctor?'

'No, Cecilia Favaro trained as a nurse, apparently, and bought the Villa Luisa to turn it into a private nursing-home, mainly for cancer patients receiving radiotherapy. She invested all her savings in it and there isn't a lot of spare cash, but she copes and there's a wonderful atmosphere here. I'll introduce you to her and show you around—but you must understand that I have to live my own life in my own way, Daddy—and right now I'm needed here.'

She spoke quietly but firmly, and Sir Peter at last realised that his daughter had made up her mind; but he was in no way reconciled to what he saw as a mad impulse on her part, probably influenced by strangers whom he distrusted.

Lucy loved her father dearly and hated to see him distressed, but she knew that this was a necessary change of direction for her if she was to regain her identity as a doctor.

When he tried to persuade her to spend a few weeks in England before starting her new job she steadfastly refused to compromise her plans, and after half an hour of fruitless argument Sir Peter left the Villa Luisa in an untypical mood of angered bewilderment. He refused to meet the *contessa*, and rejected Lucy's offer to walk back with him to his hotel.

Her conscience smote her as she watched him go, shoulders bowed and lacking the familiar jaunty spring in his step; nevertheless, she resisted the impulse to run after him and agree to reconsider her decision. Time would prove that she had done the right thing, of that she was certain.

And she was thankful to have told him and stuck to her guns; it was another hurdle overcome.

On Gabriella's balcony the atmosphere was completely transformed. The invalid reclined on her divan, her pale gold head nestling against d'Arc's shoulder and the fingers of her right hand entwined

with those of a smiling Padre Renato. Her enormous
eyes were alight with happiness as she talked animat-
edly to both men, but she broke off at the sight
of Lucy.

'Lucia, *mia cara amica*! Did I not say we were
friends from the minute we met? It is thanks to your
boldness that Findlay asks me again to marry him,
and this time I say yes! Come and let me thank you,
Lucia—*molte, molte grazie*!'

It was no time for blushing embarrassment; Lucy
hugged her friend and graciously offered her cheek
for d'Arc's kiss, as if it were all part of her day's
work to challenge a complete stranger to propose to
his mistress. She joined in the laughter when one of
Briciola's kittens tried to swing on the end of the
rope around Padre Renato's waist.

'I shall be ready and waiting to join you both in
matrimony as soon as Gabriella is out of hospital,'
promised the priest, catching Lucy's eye in acknowledgement of the part she had played in bringing him
to the Villa Luisa right on cue.

When Cecilia joined them there were more kisses
and embraces, and impromptu plans were made for
a celebratory supper.

'Is this a party?' asked a deep voice behind Lucy,
and as she turned her head Pino's lips touched her
hair; she caught her breath and inhaled a delicious
fragrance of aftershave and the warm masculine
smoothness of his skin, all in one heart-stopping
moment.

'My congratulations, *dottoressa*,' he murmured. 'It
seems that your—er—direct approach gets good
results, yes?'

'*Grazie, dottore,*' she returned demurely. 'In England it would be called barefaced cheek.'

Seven faces glowed in the candle-light that evening when a simple meal of soup, ham and cheese was served with bread and green salad on a table brought out to the balcony. The *contessa* sat opposite the newly engaged lovers, with Lucy and Pino opposite Maria and Silvio Capogna.

The sunset gave a magical touch to the wide vista of sky and sea all around them, and as the light faded outside the candles shone more brightly on the group seated at the supper table.

Findlay's eyes seldom strayed from Gabriella's face; her pale, ethereal beauty, set off by a flowing silvery-white kaftan, seemed to be illumined by an inner radiance.

Tomorrow evening she will be in a hospital bed, thought Lucy, attached to an intravenous infusion of another person's blood. She found herself hoping against all the odds that this lovely girl's health and strength might yet be restored.

Ponti must have been thinking along the same lines, for he turned and whispered in Lucy's ear.

'At a time like this we all dare to believe in miracles, do we not, Lucia?'

The closeness of this man and the intimacy of his voice set her pulses racing; she could only nod in silent agreement, and saw his sister, Maria, eyeing their little exchange from across the table. She smiled at the Capognas and made an effort to converse with them, which was not easy for they spoke no English and were painfully shy.

It occurred to Lucy again that she would never have guessed that the round-faced girl, with her swarthy husband, was the sister of the tall, fine-featured doctor, though the brother and sister were clearly close and chatted easily, referring to other members of their family.

Glasses were lifted and toasts drunk to Gabriella and her fiancé, and then Cecilia proposed an extra toast to their new resident doctor.

'As soon as she stepped across the threshold this morning, I knew that she had been sent to us,' said the *contessa*, to smiles and nods of agreement all round the table. Lucy felt her colour rising, and while she tried to compose her features Giuseppe Ponti leaned towards her and kissed her crimson cheek in front of them all.

'*Benvenuta, cara Lucia*—welcome to the Villa Luisa!' he said, and Gabriella led the round of applause that followed. Even in her blushing confusion, Lucy's shining eyes reflected the joy that welled up within her now. All the disappointments and dissatisfactions that had shadowed her life for the past two years now seemed to lift like a bank of fog dissolving in Italian sunshine.

Here, within a circle of friends that she had not even met a week ago, a new life was beginning: the Venetian summer lay ahead full of unknown experiences, and Lucy felt ready and eager to face them all.

As Pino's arm rested lightly on her shoulder she let her head fall upon his, just for a moment; it seemed so right and natural to be here beside him. When she saw Gabriella looking at her across the table she

wondered at the knowing smile on the actress's
sweet face.

What Lucy did not realise was that Gabriella could
see Pino's expression as he regarded *la bella
signorina inglese* with a new perception.

The brilliance of the violet-blue eyes and the
creamy skin of a perfect oval face, framed in dark
masses of wavy hair glinting in the soft light of the
candles, added up to a picture of breathtaking loveli-
ness, as unexpected as her challenge to d'Arc or her
acceptance of the low-paid post here at the Villa
Luisa. When she turned and met his look it was like
a moment of truth for them both. . .

Until the distant ringing of the telephone intruded
upon them like a blast of cold wind, bringing back
the real world with all its demands and complications.
Lucy felt herself tense up at the sound, and held her
breath when a nurse's face appeared at the glass door
to the balcony.

A gentleman wished to speak to 'Luceenda
Spreegsa.'

Lucy rose at once, alert and apprehensive. It could
only be her father, begging her to reconsider and
return with him tomorrow as arranged. She excused
herself from the company, determined to be firm.

But it was Aubrey Portwood's voice on the line.

'Lucinda, I think you should come over here at
once and see your father,' he said without apology
or preamble. 'I don't think he's at all well and, quite
frankly, I'm worried.'

Lucy rolled her eyes heavenward and sighed. It
seemed so obvious an attempt to get her away from
the villa so that Sir Peter and his private secretary

could use their combined powers of persuasion to make her change her mind.

'Aubrey, I've made a decision, and I know that it's been a shock to Da—to my father,' she said steadily. 'I'm terribly sorry about that, but I have my own life to lead and—'

He interrupted her with a hint of impatience.

'Just listen to me, Lucinda, will you? It's not my concern to reproach you for your treatment of Sir Peter, though I could say a great deal. I am simply telling you that I'm worried and think he should be seen by a doctor.'

Lucy made an effort to be reasonable. 'Very well, Aubrey. What exactly is the matter?'

'Well, for a start he was so upset when he returned from seeing you that I advised him to go and lie down for a couple of hours,' said Portwood accusingly. 'He didn't want any dinner this evening—only a brandy and a couple of plain biscuits. He has no appetite at all.'

Lucy felt a pang of dismay at this description of a thoroughly unhappy man. Poor Daddy.

'Does he complain of any pain?' she inquired.

'Not pain, exactly, but he's restless and unsettled. Obviously I wouldn't be ringing you if I wasn't concerned about him.'

Lucy frowned and bit her lip. It hardly sounded like an emergency, yet it could not be ignored. Just in the middle of such a wonderful evening. . .

'Are you there, Lucinda?' Portwood's voice was sharp.

'Yes, Aubrey, I'm here and I'm thinking. Look, I'll come and check him over, but—'

'Good!' he cut in. 'I shall expect you straight away.'

Lucy resented his tone, and spoke with deliberation.

'I can walk over in about fifteen minutes. And I'd better make it quite clear, Aubrey, that I'm not going to stand for any emotional blackmail. I've absolutely made up my mind to stay on here and take this job, and my father knows that.'

'I see.' His voice was cold. 'I'll be equally frank with you, Lucinda. If you are not here in fifteen minutes precisely I shall ask the manager to send for a local doctor. I have a duty to Sir Peter.'

Lucy opened her mouth to protest, but he had hung up. He had never used such a tone to her before, and it was proof of his genuine concern for his employer. A little warning shiver ran down her spine, and she hurried back to the party on the balcony to make her excuses to the *contessa*.

There was a chorus of regret and sympathy, and Pino rose from his chair. 'I'll drive you over, Lucia.'

'Oh, there's no need, thank you, Pino—I can walk there!' she protested, picturing another hostile encounter between Ponti and her father's secretary.

'Get your coat, and I'll bring the car round,' he ordered. 'The sooner you see him yourself, the better for him and you. Excuse us, Cecilia—maybe there is no cause for alarm and we shall return soon, but—' He gave a cautious shrug.

As they left the villa the telephone started ringing again.

Pino's car drew up outside the Hotel des Deux Lions just seven minutes after Lucy had taken the phone message, and they were quickly escorted up in a lift to Sir Peter's suite by a worried assistant manager.

When Lucy saw her father she felt faint. Grey-faced and perspiring, he lay on a sofa. His jacket and tie had been removed by Portwood, who was pale with anxiety himself.

'Thank God, Lucinda—when I got back from the phone he'd collapsed, and I told the manager to ring you again and also to send for an ambulance.'

Lucy was trembling all over as she knelt beside her father. Trying to feel his pulse, her hand shook so much that she could not even find it.

'Daddy—oh, Daddy, I'm sorry,' she whispered through dry lips, and it was then that a warm hand touched her shoulder and a deep voice spoke quietly in her ear.

'*Stai attenta, cara Lucia*—no talking, no crying. He needs you to be brave, yes? Let me listen to the heart.'

From that moment Ponti took complete charge. He waved Portwood aside with a smile and a polite '*Molte grazie,*' and as Lucy unbuttoned Sir Peter's shirt with shaking fingers he placed his stethoscope over the heart and listened silently for about thirty seconds, glancing at his wristwatch; then he nodded, turned down the corners of his mouth slightly and leaned over the patient, looking into eyes that stared up at him pleadingly.

'How's the pain, Sir Peter? Is it very bad?'

'Y-yes, Doctor, pretty bad—just here—I can't get my breath for it,' muttered the baronet weakly, and

Lucy turned her head aside to hide the tears that were spilling down her cheeks.

'My God, he's getting worse by the minute,' said Portwood, unable to hide his fear and anxiety. 'Anybody can see he's had a coronary thrombosis—'

'Shh, *mio amico*, do not panic; we shall need your help,' said Ponti quickly. 'You did well to send for an ambulance.'

Turning back to to Sir Peter, he spoke reassuringly.

'All right, my friend, we shall get you into the hospital here on the Lido and do some tests. *Signore*, will you get some nightclothes and bathroom things together for him? And, Lucia, check this injection, please.'

He opened the black leather bag he had brought from his car, and took out a small glass phial and a packeted sterile hypodermic syringe and needle. Lucy studied the label on the phial: diamorphine, five milligrams, and the expiry date.

She rolled up her father's sleeve and gently rubbed his upper arm with the alcohol swab that Ponti handed to her.

'This will ease your pain and make you feel nice and sleepy, Daddy,' she assured him as Ponti swiftly gave the injection.

Together they sat the patient up on pillows fetched from his bed, and as soon as he began to show signs of relief and drowsiness Ponti took his blood pressure.

'Tachycardia and hypotension,' he muttered to Lucy. 'My guess is that he's had a myocardial infarction—that would account for the degree of shock. It is the—er—*accumulazione* of acid waste in the bloodstream that causes the pain, but he is responding well to the morphine.'

He indicated her father's relaxed features and improved colour. 'Only the ECG reading will prove the diagnosis one way or another, but I have good hopes, Lucia. Be brave for him, *cara mia*,' he added with a smile, and Lucy uttered a silent prayer of thankfulness for his presence. Strength and good sense seemed to flow from him and, rather than use-lessly blame herself for what had happened, she felt her courage rising to deal with this unforeseen emergency.

She sat beside her father, holding his hand and dabbing his clammy face with a large handkerchief, while waiting for the ambulance to arrive.

'Is the pain a little better now, Daddy?' she whis-pered when he opened his eyes and looked vaguely at her.

'Better? Er—I think so, darling, a little, thank you.'

He gave her a ghost of a smile, and when she checked his pulse rate it had slowed and was slightly stronger. She sighed with relief when the ambulance drew up outside and two male attendants arrived with a stretcher-trolley onto which they slid Sir Peter with an effortlessness born of long practice.

It was decided that Lucy and Ponti should accom-pany him to the Ospedale A1 Mare, leaving Portwood in the hotel to wait for news. Once the three of them were in the ambulance Lucy turned on the portable oxygen cylinder and positioned the plastic mask over her father's nose and mouth for him to inhale.

'His colour is more pink already,' observed Ponti with an encouraging glance, and Lucy returned a rather uncertain smile. This was a different side to the man, calm and authoritative, with none of the teasing banter she had received from him since their first meeting on the second day of the Venice Convention on Cardiovascular Disorders. Was it only six days ago?

How ironic that her father was now a victim of heart disease—though, looking back, Lucy could see warning signs and her own ineffectual attempts to persuade him to take more exercise and cut down on brandies and cigars. When—Lucy shrank from saying *if*—Sir Peter recovered from this sudden calamity her warnings would have to be better heeded.

Due to the nature of the emergency, Sir Peter did not have to wait at Pronto Soccorso but was taken straight to Terapia Intensiva, where a bed was prepared to receive him. Two nurses gently removed his clothes and put on his pyjama jacket, while Lucy assisted the registrar doctor on call to connect him to an electrocardiograph monitor by means of black plastic leads, attached to his wrists and ankles and lightly strapped in place, while seven small electrodes were applied to his chest with adhesive jelly.

'I—I don't fancy having an electric current run through me,' Sir Peter muttered, and Lucy smiled.

'There's no current from the machine, Daddy. It picks up the electrical impulses coming from *you*,' she reassured him.

While the ECG tracing was in progress an intravenous infusion of dextrose saline was speedily commenced into his left arm, and the flow adjusted to forty drops a minute.

Lucy introduced herself to the duty doctor as the

patient's daughter and a qualified doctor, answering his questions on her father's behalf. Ponti was a tower of strength at her side and she noted how well-liked he was by the staff, who all seemed to know him by name.

Half an hour after admission the cardiologist confirmed that Sir Peter had suffered a partial occlusion of a coronary artery but that, with correct treatment and good general care, his chances of recovery were hopeful.

'There is good ventricular contraction, though there are occasional missed beats on the QRS complex,' he told her in Italian, with Ponti acting as interpreter for some of the technical terms. 'The dextrose drip will correct the acidosis, and I will give a diuretic to reduce the amount of fluid in his circulation.'

'And the pain?' asked Lucy anxiously. 'He seems comfortable enough now, but—'

'We shall keep him on morphine for forty-eight hours and, of course, complete bed rest,' the doctor reassured her. 'He will have continual heart monitoring and checks on his oxygen and carbon dioxide levels.' He paused, and looked directly at her as to a colleague. 'Of course, it is very early yet to make predictions, *dottoressa*, but I think you will see an improvement after twenty-four hours.'

'*Molte grazie, dottore*. Do you think it is necessary for me to stay overnight with him?'

Ponti broke in at this point, advising her to return to the Villa Luisa for the night.

'If, by any chance, you are called I shall drive you here in a matter of minutes,' he told her. 'Go and say goodnight to your father now, *cara mia*, while I telephone for a taxi.'

Lucy returned to Sir Peter's room, where a nurse was recording observations as he slept. She kissed him gently on his forehead, and as she left the coronary unit she met Valeria Corsini who had heard of the emergency admission.

'What an awful thing to happen, Lucy, just as you had made the decision to be a doctor again,' she sympathised. 'I'd drive you and Pino back to the Villa Luisa, only I'm on call. I'll look in on Sir Peter for you during the night—oh, *Lucy!*'

Whether it was her friend's affectionate hug or a reaction to all the events of a very long day, Lucy trembled and blinked back tears when Pino opened the door of the taxi for her.

'You are all right, *cara Lucia*?' he asked, getting in beside her. The driver nosed the car towards the road.

'You must think me quite useless as a doctor,' she said in a small voice. 'It was such a shock to see poor Daddy so—'

She could not continue, and covered her face with her hands. Ponti drew her close, patting her shoulder as if she were a little girl.

'I thought you did very well,' he said softly. 'It can be a great shock when a member of our own family is ill and in pain, *cara mia*, even when we are doctors and used to the sight of suffering. When my dear mother—'

He checked himself and continued, 'But you heard what the cardiologist said—your father is likely to recover, and you will feel better tomorrow when you see him better also, yes?'

She let herself be comforted by his words and the warmth of his body beside her; nestling against his arm, she found her voice again.

'I shall have to telephone Mr Portwood at his hotel—and let my mother know,' she said anxiously, thinking aloud. 'Oh, and poor Gabriella, she's going into hospital tomorrow and I promised to accompany her—'

He gave her a little shake. 'She has Findlay to be with her, and will want you to give all your time to your father. Now, I will not permit any more worrying tonight, *dottoressa*! Are you listening to me?'

She smiled up at him gratefully, and he could not resist the temptation to kiss the tip of her nose.

'*Allora*, we are here, and there is Cecilia looking out for us—I must let you go now.'

Which was fortunate, he reflected, because this was hardly a time to give way to foolish impulses with the Honourable Dr Lucia, who was continually surprising him and who was going to be living under the same roof as himself.

Unless her father's illness made her change her mind...a possibility which did not appeal to Dr Giuseppe Ponti at all.

CHAPTER SIX

AUBREY PORTWOOD was waiting for Lucy the next morning when she returned from an early visit to her father with Pino.

'I shall meet Lady Philippa at Marco Polo Airport this afternoon,' he said. 'We'll take the shuttle flight to the Lido airstrip, and get a taxi straight to the hospital. She's very upset and anxious, and wants to see Sir Peter as soon as possible.'

'Of course,' replied Lucy, who had been listening to her mother's reproaches on the phone and knew her state of mind only too well. 'Thank you, Aubrey; you've thought of everything, as usual.'

He gave a little nod. 'I've booked a room for her at the Hotel des Deux Lions,' he went on. 'I must return to London tomorrow, much as I'd like to stay on, but things will need sorting out in the office. I've telephoned Miss Elstone and told her I shall need her tomorrow evening—she's had an easy time lately and there'll be a huge backlog of reports, correspondence and so on.'

He paused and looked questioningly at Lucy.

'Er—I presume that you will change your plans now, Lucinda, and return home with Sir Peter as soon as he is fit enough, whenever that may be.'

'Not necessarily, Aubrey. It depends on how he progresses. He was looking very much better this morning, and I told him that my mother's on her way. Will you tell her that I hope to be with him when she arrives?'

He sighed, and Lucy noticed how pale and drawn he looked. On an impulse she stepped forward and gave him a quick kiss on the cheek.

'Thank you for everything, Aubrey. You've been marvellous. I do appreciate it, you know—truly I do.'

'There is nothing I would not do for you, Lucinda.'

'I know. And now if you'll excuse me, the ambulances will be here soon to take four of our guests across the Lagoon—*arrivederci*!'

'Goodbye until this afternoon, Lucinda.'

Gabriella's belongings were packed ready for her admission to the Ospedale Civile, and d'Arc was at her side. She held Lucy close in a farewell hug.

'We are so sorry about your father, *cara* Lucia— Pino told me that you and he have seen him again this morning. I wish there was something we could do—Findlay will send him flowers from both of us, and you know you have all our good wishes.'

Lucy was touched at her friend's concern at such a time, and by the card she had received from all the staff. The ambulances were waiting, and as soon as Gabriella had gone and the other guests had embarked for their radiotherapy in the care of two nurses Lucy went in search of Maria Capogna.

She tracked her down in the kitchen, happily peeling and slicing vegetables.

'Maria! You know that the contessa will be cross if she finds you working here!'

Maria rolled up her black button eyes and held out her plump arms in a gesture of total boredom.

'*La vita è molta tediosa!*' she wailed, and went on to complain in voluble Italian that without Gabriella there would be nothing to occupy her time, and that she was tired of sitting around and putting on weight—which Signore d'Arc had said she must not do.

Lucy smiled, feeling that the girl had a point.

'Come into the surgery and let's have a talk,' she suggested, seeing an opportunity to do a full antenatal and general check, while asking a few discreet questions about the family history.

The scales showed a depressing seventy-six kilograms, though Maria protested that she kept strictly to the high-protein, low-carbohydrate diet ordered for her.

'Are you sure, Maria? Do you eat nothing else at all?'

The girl pouted. 'Well, sometimes my Silvio worries about me when I wake up in the night feeling hungry,' she admitted with a pathetic air. 'He says his baby must not starve, so he brings me chocolate and biscuits.'

Lucy decided that tact was needed here. To scold Maria might make her sulky, and to tell Ponti or the contessa about her nocturnal feasts would lose her trust. She held up a reproving forefinger.

'Maria, *cara*, you know that is not a good idea, and I will have to speak to Silvio,' she said in careful Italian. 'It's important that you do not carry too much weight and also this is very bad for your teeth, which decay quickly when you are carrying a baby. Now, what can we do about this hunger at night? What about a drink of fortified milk when you go to bed?'

She named a product that the guests were given, and while Maria thought it over Lucy recorded her pulse—one hundred and eight—and respirations—thirty-two per minute—both quite high, considering that she had only walked a few yards with no stairs to climb.

'Are you making any clothes for your baby, Maria?' she asked. 'What about knitting a nice cot-blanket in bright colours?'

'I could crochet squares in different coloured wool, and sew them together,' said Maria with a glimmer of interest.

'Oh, what a good idea! I'm sure you could think of some really pretty patterns,' smiled Lucy, thinking that it would be something Maria could pick up and put down when she felt like it. 'Like doing a jigsaw puzzle,' she added, hoping to relieve the girl's boredom. 'You've nearly got to thirty-two weeks now, so not much longer to go; in fact, you're doing very well—so I'll just have a word with Silvio about the—'

'*I* will tell him, *dottoressa*—no more eating in bed!'

Maria grinned broadly, and Lucy had to smile.

'Tell me about this rheumatic fever you had when you were a child, Maria.'

'I don't remember much about it, but Dr Corsini says it's the reason for my weak heart. Pino got Signore d'Arc to see me, and that is why I am getting so lazy from doing nothing,' replied Maria with a shrug.

'How are your parents?' Lucy asked casually as

she helped to heave the girl's bulky body onto the examination couch.

'Our mother died three years ago,' answered Maria mournfully. 'She never complained that she was feeling ill until one day Pino made her go to the hospital, and then it was too late to save her. Pino was very angry with himself for not noticing sooner—but he lived away from home, and we are all to blame for not seeing that poor Mamma was so ill. It makes me sad that she will not see my baby.'

Lucy remembered how Pino had cut himself off in mid-sentence when speaking of his mother, and could imagine his bitter regret.

'And your father—is he well?' she asked gently.

'Oh, yes, he is on the *vaporetti*, and says he is like Pino—making money from the tourists!'

Lucy cleared her throat discreetly.

'But Pino is much cleverer than the rest of us,' added Maria.

He must be, thought Lucy, to have risen from such humble origins to become a qualified doctor. Maria went on chatting, saying that her two other brothers were boatmen and a sister kept house for them and their father.

As Lucy palpated Maria's abdomen and ascertained that the baby was active and growing well, she wondered if Pino had won some kind of award to assist him through medical school. There was so much she wanted to know about this Venetian doctor whose background was in such stark contrast to her own—but with whom she would be working on an equal professional footing.

However, she reminded herself that this was no

time for idle speculation; her father was lying ill in hospital, and her mother flying out to be at his side. The guests would soon be returning from their radiotherapy, fatigued and perhaps depressed and nauseated, needing individual attention and a listening ear. This might not be a busy NHS hospital like Beltonshaw General but there were many demands upon her time and energy, and Lucy knew that she could not afford to fail.

Lady Philippa Hallcross-Spriggs embraced her daughter in the corridor of Terapia Intensiva.

'What a dreadful thing to happen, Lucinda! Thank heaven you have had Aubrey with you—such a tower of strength!'

'Yes, he's been very good,' replied Lucy a little awkwardly, as Portwood was standing beside them. 'Now, we mustn't let our feelings show, Mummy—it's most important to keep quiet and calm in front of Daddy.'

She opened the door of Sir Peter's room. He was sitting propped up on a bank of pillows, the cardiac monitor screen above the bed, the intravenous drip in his left arm and a bladder drainage bag at the side of the bed. His face lit up at the sight of his wife and daughter, and when greetings and kisses had been exchanged Aubrey was invited in to see the invalid's improvement on the previous evening.

'I'm to sit out of bed tomorrow, and if I'm a good boy they say I can do a little polka round the room,' said the baronet with a touch of his former jauntiness. 'Everybody's very kind here but, of course, they don't understand a word I say!'

After ten minutes Lucy told her parents that she would leave them alone together.

'I've got patients to see,' she explained.

'But surely not more important than your father?'

'Of course not, but I have a commitment to them. I'll meet you again later, Mummy, and we'll have a good talk.'

She kissed her father's cheek and whispered, 'You're doing fine, Daddy; keep up the good work!'—and escaped before Lady Philippa could remonstrate further.

When she reached the Villa Luisa more problems awaited.

'Grazie al Signore!' cried Cecilia as Lucy ran up the front steps. 'We have an emergency, *cara mia*. Giuseppino had an urgent call to go to a hotel where half the guests are sick and in pain—some of them quite bad. It sounds like food poisoning, but could be an infection—the manager is going mad.'

'How awful!' Lucy was immediately concerned. 'Does Dr Ponti need any help?'

'Certamente! But the help is needed here, Lucia, when his patients arrive for evening surgery. There will be no one to see them—I cannot get a substitute doctor. Lucia, can you possibly take this surgery so that I need not turn them away?'

Lucy stood very still, returning Cecilia's distracted gaze. She was being asked to see a series of patients whom she did not know, men and women of all ages with a variety of problems—serious and trivial. They would speak to her in a foreign language, complicated by the Venetian dialect, and wait for her reactions, her suggestions and advice. She was not sure that she could do them justice.

'I'm willing to take Dr Ponti's surgery, Cecilia, but the biggest problem is language,' she replied after a long pause. 'This is such an intimate, personal thing for them, and if I can't communicate properly—'

The contessa's worried frown disappeared at once.

'*Molte grazie*, Lucia! You will take the surgery, and I will interpret for you when necessary, yes? *Va bene!*'

Sending up a silent but heartfelt prayer, Lucy went into Pino's surgery and donned a white coat several sizes too large for her. She took down a stethoscope from its hook and put it round her neck; Cecilia bustled around with case-cards and put out a prescription pad and request forms for X-rays and laboratory examinations. The surgery was due to begin at five-thirty, and there were already three patients in the waiting-room.

'All right, *contessa*, please send the first one in,' said Lucy, assuming a confident air that she was far from feeling.

The first patient was a house-painter in his fifties who had pain and stiffness in his left shoulder, which made it difficult for him to work, being left-handed. His neck movements were normal and there was no numbness of his arm, though he winced when asked to raise his arm above his head. Lucy thought he had probably strained a muscle, but listened to his heart to exclude anginal pain.

She prescribed an analgesic and asked him to come back in a week if the pain was no better, in which case she suggested he might try a spinal collar.

The next was a tired-looking housewife with persistent frontal headaches. It appeared that she augmented her husband's low income by sewing for a dressmaker, often late at night after her five children were in bed. Lucy advised a visit to an optician and tried to impress on the woman the need for sufficient sleep, though it was all too clear that poverty and her husband's drinking were the root causes of her symptoms.

The patients came and went in a steady stream: a mother with eight-year-old twins who coughed in unison; a woman with vague digestive problems who complained bitterly about her husband's neglect of her; a boatman with varicose ulcers; a young man with an untreated knee injury from football, now beginning to give him pain and disability; a *pensione* manageress worried about her overweight, unhappy, fifteen-year-old daughter—about half of them had symptoms related to emotional or social problems. It seemed that there were unhappy marriages, unsuitable jobs and rebellious youngsters even here on the Lido of Venice.

An hour and a half had passed, and Lucy began to feel a sense of achievement. She had coped, and Cecilia was delighted.

'*Meravigliosa!* I will go to make coffee—we both deserve it, Lucia!'

Left alone, Lucy found herself facing one more patient—a late arrival who dashed into the surgery and sat down opposite her. He was a good-looking young man, casually but expensively dressed, and he was clearly very worried.

'I am not a local resident, *dottoressa*. I was hoping

to see a male doctor, but if you can tell me what is wrong and what can be done about it—'

'Very well, I will try,' replied Lucy, reaching for a new case-card. 'Your name, please? Address? Date of birth?'

Vittorio Goldoni was twenty-five and gave a Milan address. He said he was a trainee executive with a car firm. In describing his symptoms he was much less precise, saying that he had felt vaguely unwell for the past couple of months with little appetite or energy. 'I have lost three kilograms,' he told Lucy.

'How well do you sleep?' she asked.

'Not very well—I wake up soaked in perspiration some nights, and feel feverish and shivery. I thought I had influenza, but it just will not go away,' he said wearily.

'You say you're not married—' Lucy hesitated, finding it difficult to ask an intimate question in Italian. 'But you have friends, I am sure—er—girl-friends?'

'Sure, like everybody else!' He nodded and shrugged.

'Have you had any recent illnesses or—er—infections?'

'Not that I know of, *dottoressa*—only this one.'

Lucy considered the meagre information before her. This could be so many things. Glandular fever was a possibility, or the onset of a serious inflammatory disease such as hepatitis or endocarditis. Tuberculosis would fit the symptoms, but that was most unlikely in a man of his obvious affluence.

'Take off your jacket and shirt, *signore*.'

As she listened carefully to his heart and lungs she

noted his general condition; he had a few acne spots
on his skin, and his muscle tone had diminished with
his loss of weight. Putting down the stethoscope, she
felt his neck and armpits, pressing gently with her
fingertips; then she got him to lie down on the couch,
and examined his abdomen and groin in the
same way.

'There is a small swelling at the back of your neck,
signore,' she said at last, sitting down at the desk
while he readjusted his clothes. 'How long have you
had it?'

He had neither noticed nor felt it.

'Well, you're going to need some investigations
done, *signore*, and soon,' she told him firmly. 'I'll
send you to the Ospedale Civile for a batch of blood
tests and X-rays, including a special X-ray called a
lymphangiogram—and a biopsy of that lump. They
might have to admit you for a day because you'll
need an anaesthetic.'

'OK, no problem.' His face was tense. 'How soon
could all these things be done?'

'I'll telephone a friend of mine, a Dr Scogliera,
and ask if he can see you tomorrow,' she said.

'Molte grazie, dottoressa.' He closed his eyes and
clasped his hands together. 'So—what do you
think it is?'

'I'm not sure,' she temporised. 'We shall have to
wait for the results, and take it from there.'

'If it's Aids I'll die, won't I?'

It was a statement rather than a question, and Lucy
chose her next words carefully.

'Let's not rush to conclusions, Vittorio. An HIV
test will be included with the rest, and Dr Scogliera

won't keep you waiting any longer than necessary. When we've got a diagnosis you'll be referred to the appropriate specialist.'

She stood up and held out her hand. 'Good luck! *Buona fortuna!*'

As Cecilia brought in the coffee Ponti rushed through the door, jacketless and with his hair wildly on end.

'Lucia! I am so sorry to leave you with all this—how did it go?'

'Eccellente!' cried Cecilia, and Lucy smiled.

'I don't think I could have managed without Cecilia. I've just had a very difficult interview in Italian—I wish you could have seen this young man, Pino.'

He glanced at the case-card. 'Goldoni—Milano. Hmm.'

'He said he works in the family car firm. Actually, Pino, I think he came here to avoid letting his family know.'

Ponti grimaced. 'Why, has he been a naughty boy?'

'He's terrified that he might have Aids, but I found this sinister lump in his neck and wondered about lymphoma—Hodgkin's disease—do you call it that?'

'O mio Dio! What did you do with him, Lucia?'

She told him the investigations she had requested, and her promise to contact Scogliera. 'If it is Hodgkin's, he'd better be referred straight to Oncology, I thought.'

Ponti nodded his agreement, and stared at the case-card.

'Goldoni. . . .you know, Lucia, he could be the son and heir of Diva—Diva Macchine, the big car manufacturers. In which case he is not short of a few billion lire.'

He frowned, and Lucy noticed that he and Cecilia exchanged a significant look. 'He might as well have gone to a doctor in Milano.'

'But he didn't *want* to go to the family doctor, Pino; that was the whole point of making the journey.'

'My dear Lucia, this young man will have to face facts. If he has a life-threatening disease, Aids or Hodgkin's, he won't be able to hide it for much longer.'

'Poor boy,' murmured Cecilia, finishing her coffee and piling the cups on the tray.

When she'd left them Ponti sat on the side of the desk, drumming his fingers on the surface.

'Lucia, I must ask you this—will your father's illness make any difference to your plans?'

'I've been thinking about that for the past twenty-four hours, Pino, even in my sleep,' she confessed. 'It depends on Daddy's progress. If he continues to do well he could be discharged in a couple of weeks, and then I will have to accompany him on the flight home.'

'I thought as much,' he said flatly.

'That is the least I can do for him, Pino. But I shall return to my work here as soon as possible.'

His dark eyes lit up with undisguised relief.

'*Grazie, amore mio! Meravigliosa!* Cecilia will be so pleased; she has been worrying her head off about it! And so have I.'

He leaned eagerly towards her across the desk, and she was conscious of a quickening of her heartbeat.

'Believe me, Pino, I don't intend to leave the Villa Luisa until I have worked out my contract,' she said, trying to keep her voice even. 'Though I hope I don't get landed too often with your surgery!'

'Ah, but how well you did it, Lucia, yes? We could be a perfect partnership, you looking after the guests and me—er—making the "rich pickings" out of the tourists—that is what you said, is it not?'

His dark eyes were teasing her, but there was something more in their depths which made Lucy's breath quicken with her pulse. She tried to speak lightly.

'Oh, don't remind me! Though perhaps you deserved it for trying to show me up in front of all those delegates!'

'But you won, Lucia—you shot me down in flames, remember?'

He came round the desk towards her, speaking in a lowered tone, his eyes locked with hers so that she could not turn away.

'And I have been burning ever since, no matter how I try to cool myself. You are always there in my thoughts, Lucia. Your face, your so English voice, your—ah, you are such a beautiful woman, and I cannot—*non posso*—'

It happened so quickly, so naturally. When he laid his hand on her shoulder she covered it with her own. And then they were together, their arms around each other in a breathless embrace.

'Oh, Pino,' she heard herself whisper as his lips touched her hair, her forehead, her cheek, her neck— and when at last he found her soft mouth, her lips parted for him with all the ardour of a woman ready for love. They clung together in an aching, overwhelming release of emotion, all reservations swept away on the tide that had so swiftly engulfed them.

'Pino, oh, Pino.' She gave a bliss-filled sigh when at last he released her lips to draw breath. She felt his heart hammering in rhythm with her own, and her breasts strained beneath her silk blouse and the oversize white coat.

He muttered incoherently, in mixed English and Italian, 'Did not intend to—with your father ill—to take advantage of you—*questo non è corretto*—I try to hold back—'

These half-apologies thrilled Lucy all the more, sending her thoughts whirling to heights of incredulous joy. She experienced again that sense of destiny, of homecoming, that she had felt before in this man's arms when they had stood outside the Ospedale Al Mare in the evening of the day they had met—and in St Mark's Square among the dancers, when he had rescued her and told her she was safe.

Yes! With this man beside her she could face any challenge, deal with any emergency that arose. Gone were her resolutions to keep him at arm's length. Every nerve tingled, every muscle trembled in response to his body, hard against hers. She was falling, melting, drowning in his arms. . .

Yet it was she who first heard the footsteps approaching the surgery door, and the sound of a man and a woman talking.

'Pino—Pino, stop—*stop*!'

Unclasping her hands from behind his neck, she pushed him away from her and he almost groaned aloud as she released herself. It was only just in time.

'Lucinda!'

Pino found himself gaping at an older version of the woman he had just been holding in his arms— the same shape of face, the same deep blue eyes, the same cultured English voice. *O mio Dio*, he thought, there is no need to be introduced. Portwood hovered behind her, stony-eyed.

Lucy held up her head, smoothing her hands over the white coat and pushing back a stray lock of dark hair.

'Hello, Mummy.' Her voice was amazingly steady. 'This is Dr Giuseppe Ponti, who was such a support to me last night when Daddy was taken ill.'

Pino managed a little bow, and was rewarded by a haughty stare from Lady Philippa.

'I've come to ask you to join us for dinner at our hotel, Lucinda. How soon can you be ready?'

Lucy braced herself.

'Thank you, Mummy, but I can't manage this evening,' she said pleasantly. 'And you surely need an early night after all your travelling. Let's make it tomorrow evening, shall we?'

'But Aubrey has to return to London tomorrow!' Lady Philippa protested.

'I'm sorry, Mummy, but I have ill patients who need me to be available for them,' said Lucy quietly.

Lady Philippa's imperious arched eyebrows rose, but she heard the finality in Lucy's words and decided not to risk losing face in undignified argument.

'Very well,' she said icily, 'but I shall speak to you later, Lucinda.'

And, taking Portwood's arm, she turned and swept out of the surgery without another word.

Lucy turned to Ponti, her face flushed.

'Sorry about that, Pino. Not the best of introductions.'

'*O, mi dispiace!*' he groaned. 'I am full of regret, Lucia!'

'It was no more your fault than mine,' she replied briskly, vexed beyond measure that their moment of closeness had passed, leaving her with a slightly embarrassing sense of anticlimax. Oh, why on earth did her mother have to appear just at that moment?

'Families are funny, aren't they, Pino?' she remarked in an attempt to ease the tension between them. 'Your sister was telling me about yours today. I was very sorry to hear about your mother.'

'Yes, she was a good woman who suffered much in her life,' he said sombrely, and Lucy sensed a continuing unresolved grief. She longed to hear more—to get to the heart of the mystery that surrounded this man who had so suddenly, so amazingly invaded her life and turned it upside down. But time was getting on, and she was due to do her evening round of the guests.

'I shall have to go now, Pino,' she said a little shyly, adding with a smile, 'I'd better let you have your white coat back! Oh, and you must let me know what happens about that young man I saw!'

He assured her that he would and so the moment passed, leaving Lucinda wondering if his emotions were in as much turmoil as her own.

But inwardly she hugged her secret joy, for in that moment Lucy finally acknowledged that she had at last come through her heartbreak over David Rowan.

And into the blinding light of a new love. . .

*   *   *

The days flew by and April arrived, as warm as an English June. Sir Peter made excellent progress and by the end of a week he was transferred to a medical ward, where he was able to walk to the bathroom and eat his meals at a table with the other patients. The cardiologist was delighted with him.

'His serum enzyme levels are almost back to normal, showing that the infarct is healing,' he told Lucy. 'He's taking all his medication by mouth now—I'm keeping him on anticoagulants and beta blockers, though there's no arrhythmia.

'His worst problem is boredom, I'm afraid, especially as he can't understand what anybody's saying! If he were near his home he could be discharged and take things quietly, but he's not yet ready for a two-hour flight, is he?'

Lady Philippa broke in at this point.

'But he can surely come back to the hotel with me! There's an excellent room service and every possible comfort.'

Lucy sighed. She had already arranged with Cecilia for Sir Peter to stay at the Villa Luisa as soon as he was considered fit. She braced herself yet again for another confrontation.

'He'll have proper nursing care at the villa, Mummy, and I'll be on the spot for him at any time, day or night.'

'My husband needs a hopeful atmosphere, not to be surrounded by terminal invalids,' retorted Lady Philippa.

The matter was settled when the hotel manager politely but firmly refused to accept his former guest after the panic of his heart seizure. It was a hotel, not a hospital, and his staff were not trained in coronary care, he explained.

Sir Peter was accordingly given a double room at the Villa Luisa, and Lady Philippa graciously accepted Cecilia's cordial invitation to move in with her husband. He settled well in the friendly, homelike atmosphere, and Lucy noticed that he had grown more reflective as a result of his experience.

Pino also remarked on his change of attitude.

'I have been watching your father as he sees you going about your daily routine here, Lucia,' he told her over a hurried lunch they were sharing at the end of a busy morning. 'He now is beginning to realise that his darling daughter is also a competent doctor, well liked by everybody, yes?'

There was a special tenderness in the look he gave her as he said this that made her blush with something more than mere pleasure at such praise from a fellow professional.

'We've both changed, Pino,' she replied simply. 'I respect him tremendously for his courage and determination to recover from the blow he's had. We've got a more realistic relationship altogether now.'

Lady Philippa was a different matter, however. Impressed by Cecilia's title of Countess, the baronet's wife treated her as an equal but the nurses resented her imperious tones ringing through the Villa, ordering them around like servants. Lucy was guiltily relieved when a further outbreak of gastroenteritis at a second hotel on the Lido kept Ponti out at all hours and therefore out of earshot of her ladyship.

But one morning when he dashed into the dispensary to pick up a further supply of dioralyte solution he heard upraised voices by the lifts, and found a tearful and panting Maria holding her abdomen as she leaned against the wall.

Rushing to her side, he heard that '*la madre di Lucia*' had commandeered the lift for Sir Peter and had not allowed Maria to share it.

'She told me to walk upstairs because the exercise will do me good,' Maria gasped, clinging to her indignant brother.

It was too much. Ponti leapt up the stairs two at a time in search of her ladyship, and burst onto Sir Peter's balcony where the couple sat. Lucy was on the adjoining balcony with a patient, out of sight but able to hear every word.

'I want a word with you, *signora*,' Ponti began without ceremony. 'My sister is pregnant and has a serious heart condition. On no account is she to climb stairs and you must never upset her again—she must always use the lift. Is that quite clear to you?'

Anybody else would have quailed before the doctor's blazing eyes, but Lady Philippa merely shrugged and raised her eyebrows.

'If that girl has got a heart condition, Doctor, I am surprised you have allowed her to put on so much weight. She's nearly as broad as she's long, and don't tell me that can be good for her.'

Ponti was about to give an angry retort when he caught sight of Sir Peter's worried frown. Not wanting to cause the baronet emotional stress, the doctor contented himself with a final glare at Lady Philippa and strode off to Cecilia's office.

Lucy followed him quietly at a safe distance, and stood outside the door.

'Insufferable woman!' she heard him explode in Italian. 'How I would like to wring her neck! To speak to Maria in that way. Poor old Peter, I pity him, being married to such a—'

Lucy cringed and felt she could have died from shame as she crept away. At her earliest opportunity she tackled her mother, trying to explain that the contessa liked to maintain an informal atmosphere with staff and guests on an equal footing.

'Don't try to excuse these people to me, Lucinda,' replied her mother coldly. 'Quite frankly, I'm surprised to know that your precious Dr Ponti is brother to that lump of a girl. Talk about a peasant! Oh, I know they're good enough people but I think the countess makes far too much fuss of them. Now, Lucinda, look at this charming letter from dear Aubrey—'

Lucy gave up, and could only hope that Sir Peter would soon be fit to fly home.

On the following afternoon Lucy and Valeria Corsini made the trip across the Lagoon to visit Gabriella. The actress looked as fragile as ever, but said that she was feeling stronger after the transfusion of six half-litres of blood.

'I am just living for the day of my return to the villa and my wedding to Findlay,' she told them serenely.

Gianni Scogliera joined them at the bedside, and spoke to Lucy about another patient in that department—Vittorio Goldoni.

'Your diagnosis was not far out, Lucia,' he said. 'The good news is that he is HIV negative, and the bad is that he has lymphoma, stage I.'

Lucy was all concern. 'What does the professor suggest?'

'Hit him hard with megavoltage radiotherapy daily for five weeks. There's a good survival rate if it's tackled early and the professor's quite optimistic, though of course it will knock the stuffing out of him, poor chap. Would you like to see him?'

As soon as Goldoni saw Lucy he held out both hands to her.

'*Dottoressa!* You are the very person I want to see—you and the Contessa Favaro. Let's get to business!'

It appeared that young Goldoni was indeed the heir to Diva Macchine di Milano and was anxious to keep his illness secret—away from the paparazzi.

'I am having daily radiotherapy here and, although this private room is OK, I'd rather hide myself at the Villa Luisa. I will pay whatever the contessa requires.'

'But it will be very exhausting for you to travel across the Lagoon every day, Vittorio,' said Lucy. 'With the high dosage you are receiving, you will—'

'I know, but I would prefer it, *dottoressa*, and if you can arrange for me to move in at the weekend I shall be grateful. Knowing that I have not got—that other terrible disease, I can put up with feeling lousy for a while!'

Lucy thought quickly. If her parents could return to England at the weekend then Goldoni could move into their room and peace would once again descend upon the Villa Luisa—but she could scarcely be spared to accompany her parents on the flight. She mentioned the problem to Valeria.

'Oh, Lucia, you have given me a wonderful idea!' said her friend with shining eyes. 'Gianni is off to London on Saturday for a seminar at the Royal Marsden Hospital. It doesn't start till Monday, and if *I* were to accompany Sir Peter and see him safely home there'd still be Sunday to—er—'

Lucy chuckled at Valeria's deviousness. 'It sounds like a brilliant idea,' she agreed. 'Let's see what we can do!'

The cardiologist pronounced Sir Peter well enough to travel by air, but even Lucy was unprepared for her mother's reaction when she heard that their daughter was not coming with them.

'It was bad enough to worry your father into a coronary thrombosis, Lucinda, without deserting him altogether when he needs you most,' she said bitterly. 'You call yourself a doctor, and yet you—'

'Mummy, that's not fair,' protested Lucy, deeply hurt. 'You will have an experienced doctor with you—what more do you want? How many times have I to remind you that I have *work* to do here? Daddy understands this now, so why can't you?'

'Your father has been too indulgent with you, Lucinda, and now the poor man's paying for it!' stormed Lady Philippa. 'Oh, I'm not blind, I can see what the attraction is here. It's that Dr Ponti, isn't it? It seems to be a failing with you, Lucinda, to fall for unsuitable men—first there was that ghastly doctor at Beltonshaw who threw you over to marry a tart of a midwife, and now you've got entangled with an upstart who manipulates you just as he manipulates the poor countess. And, by what I've heard, you're by no means the only one to fall for him!'

'*Mother!*' Lucy went pale and closed her eyes.

'You've been a disappointment to us, Lucinda.' Lady Philippa's voice broke on a sob. 'But we still love you because you're our daughter. Just remember that when this Ponti throws you over, and then you'll be glad to come home again!'

She wiped her eyes. 'And we'll be willing to have you back, Lucinda, even though you've treated us so badly.'

There seemed to be no answer to this parting shot. Sir Peter kissed his daughter and pressed her hand in wordless sympathy. Ponti was out on his rounds when the couple left by taxi for the Lido airstrip with Dr Corsini, and Lucy wondered wretchedly if this had been deliberate on his part. She noticed the smiles on the faces of the staff.

Heavens, she thought, can that be how I came across to the nurses at St Margaret's and Beltonshaw General?

Cecilia put an arm around her and whispered, 'It has been a pleasure to have your father here, *cara mia*, and we are all so glad he is better.'

She took an envelope from her pocket. 'And look here—he has authorised his bank to pay ten million lire to the Villa Luisa!'

Lucy gasped. It was the equivalent of almost five thousand pounds sterling, a very welcome addition to the *contessa's* depleted funds.

She felt Pino's arm thrown around her shoulders and heard his deep voice in her ear, explaining how the money would be used.

'This means she can have the exterior repaired and repainted, thanks to your father's generosity, Lucia,' he smiled. 'It means such a lot to her.'

Lucy's eyes were suddenly misty. It was Daddy's way of saying that he understood her need to live her own life, and that he forgave her for the distress she had caused him.

She returned Pino's smile in anticipation of sharing ideas and opinions about their work and drawing ever closer; she longed to hear him call her *amore mio* again.

However, neither she nor anybody else at the Villa Luisa saw much of him for a while; the outbreak of enteritis continued to rage, and he was called out at all hours. The death of an elderly American tourist brought about a state of emergency, and the Department of Health introduced temporary measures for the control of infection.

Pino took up residence at one of the two hotels affected by the epidemic, and was engulfed in an avalanche of paperwork, as he told Lucy on the phone.

'I still think this is food poisoning, probably a virulent strain of salmonella, but the hotel proprietors are trying to blame it on water pollution,' he said. 'Many samples must be taken before we can be sure and, meanwhile, I had better keep away from the Villa Luisa.' He added that the daughter of the manageress at the second hotel was quite poorly, and that he did not like to leave her.

'I know that girl; her name is Gianetta,' said Cecilia with a significant look. 'She has been chasing Giuseppino ever since he took her out in his *motoscafo* last year. This will give her an opportunity to entice him into her room, yes?'

Lucy frowned, remembering the light-hearted gossip between Valeria and Gianni about Pino's conquests at the Venice Film Festival, and felt a pang of unease; although she told herself not to be so silly about a seriously sick young woman, a nagging little imp of doubt remained at the back of her mind, and the Contessa's words came back to her from time to time. . .

A locum was found to take the surgeries and do the essential house calls but Lucy and Cecilia were kept busy with the residents, who now included young Goldoni. His daily journeys to the intensive radiotherapy sessions left him utterly debilitated, and he spent most of his time resting. He had told the *contessa* that he would not be having any visitors.

Until one afternoon when Cecilia had gone to visit Gabriella, and Lucy was in charge.

CHAPTER SEVEN

'*MI SCUSI, dottoressa*—there is a gentleman to see Vittorio.'

Lucy was surprised, and said that she would have a word with the visitor. The staff had instructions not to speak to anybody about Goldoni, and so far there had been no inquiries about him; Lucy presumed that he had given his family some plausible reason for his long absence from home.

When she saw the tall, grey-haired man waiting in the reception room she was prepared to be on the defensive, shielding her guest from any intrusion upon his privacy. She was a little taken aback when the man rose and gave her a courtly little bow.

She judged him to be about sixty, with dark, deep-set eyes and features hardened by experience and suffering. Two vertical lines between his thick brows were matched by permanently etched furrows from his nose to the corners of his mouth. There was a nobility about his bearing, but Lucy sensed that he was not a happy man.

'*Buongiorno, signore. Sono Dr Spriggs, e sono inglese. Le posso aiutare?* How can I help you?' she asked.

'*Buongiorno*, Dr Spriggs. I speak a little English,' he replied with a smile and Lucy warmed towards him, though she maintained her formal professional manner and waited for him to speak.

136

'*Allora!* I believe that my godson, Vittorio Goldoni, is staying here?'

'Signore Goldoni is a guest here, yes,' she affirmed. 'But he has particularly requested that he is not to be visited, and in any case he is resting at present.'

He nodded and looked grave. 'I am sorry for that, Dr Spriggs. I was hoping that he would consent to see his—er—*zio* Faro, his uncle Faro—it is what he called me when he was a little boy. Is it possible that he can be told I am here?'

Lucy asked him to wait while she spoke to Goldoni.

The young man was lying on his bed with the curtains drawn, a bowl and a glass of soda water at his bedside. He raised his head when he heard the door click.

'Vittorio, there is a gentleman to see you. He says he is your godfather, your *zio* Faro.'

'*Mio zio Faro!*' he said in surprise. 'How did he find me? All right, Dr Lucia, send him in.'

At the end of half an hour Lucy knocked on the door to ask the visitor to leave. He thanked her politely for making an exception in his case, and as they walked to the lifts he assured her that he would not reveal Goldoni's hiding-place.

'I will let his parents know that he is safe and being well cared for,' he told her. 'They have been frantic with worry, as you may imagine, Dr Spriggs. I am an old friend of his father, and I have done a little detective-work through—er—Vittorio's bank, you understand.'

Lucy felt it her duty to warn him not to raise the parents' hopes too high.

'He has a serious condition, *signore*, and the treatment is very debilitating.'

'So I observe, *dottoressa*—but it is not what he feared, no?'

'No, *signore*.'

When they emerged from the lift he hesitated for a moment, and then asked abruptly, 'How is Contessa Favaro?'

'Very well,' replied Lucy. 'She is visiting in Venice today.'

'I see.' He sighed heavily. 'Just as well, perhaps.'

'Shall I tell her you asked after her, *signore*?'

'No, I think not, Dr Spriggs, thank you. You have been very kind. This is a beautiful place for poor young Vittorio to stay.'

'Molte grazie, signore.'

They shook hands, and she watched his upright figure go down the steps and out between the stone lions. She wondered what his connection with the *contessa* could be: a romantic affair of the past? Lucy felt strangely drawn to the man for a reason she could not define.

Cecilia was full of news about Gabriella on her return.

'She is due for discharge to us at the weekend, and wants to be married within days of her return,' she informed Lucy. 'Findlay is in Paris, tying up loose ends of his work there so that he can move to Venice and devote all his time to her. I must tell Padre Renato, and there will be all kinds of preparations to make, yes?

'I have promised Gabriella a reception here in the garden of the Villa Luisa—her parents will come from Padua, and his from England— *O mio Dio!*'

Lucy foresaw a very busy time ahead. With Pino still involved with the enteritis outbreak, she was already working at full stretch. The needs of seriously ill guests, as much emotional as medical, constantly challenged her ingenuity, and she was gaining a whole new perspective on this particular area of her profession.

On the Friday afternoon of that week Lucy flopped into a basket chair on the back veranda, intending to take a fifteen-minute break with a cup of tea.

She lay back and closed her eyes, letting her limbs relax, and drifted into a delicious doze in which Pino's face was close to hers. So close that their lips were almost touching. She smiled, willing the dream to continue and not fade away. His lips were upon hers. . .she sighed with pleasure as he kissed her. . . It felt so real.

So real! Lucy's eyes snapped open, and there he was before her—the kiss was no dream!

'Pino! It—it's really you! Are you back with us again now?' she asked in happy confusion.

'*Si, mia bella Lucia,*' he replied, kissing her again, and, taking the chair beside her, he held her hand while his dark eyes looked deeply into hers for a long moment. Lucy longed to lean across and lay her head upon his shoulder, but knew that she must not give way to any such basic impulse. Smoothing back her hair with a quick gesture, she asked him the latest news of the outbreak.

'I'd rather talk about you, Lucia *mia*, but to sit here beside you must be enough pleasure for me, yes?' She noticed the tiredness in his face and the hollows under his eyes from lack of sleep, but there was no mistaking his pleasure in her company.

'The causative organism has been isolated and traced to contaminated shellfish, so the hotels are still trying to pass the buck to the water authority,' he told her with a wry grimace. 'I had to give evidence at the inquest on the tourist—poor old man—and found myself caught in the crossfire. All the other victims are now recovering—except for the hotel proprietors, who have lost much business!'

'And the daughter of the manageress—the lovely Gianetta—has she also recovered?' inquired Lucy casually.

'Ah, happily she is improving now, but she really had me worried for a day or two, poor girl.' He smiled. *'Allora!* Venice has been plagued all through her history with water-borne epidemics, and we must be thankful it was not cholera, no? Now, Lucia, *cara*, tell me what has been happening here. How is Maria?'

'Everything seems all right antenatally, but her pulse and respiration rates shoot up during any exertion. Her weight has been static for the past two weeks,' she reported, knowing that the nocturnal chocolate orgies had stopped.

'I worry about her,' he admitted. 'It's why I kept away from here during the outbreak. Any infection would go straight to her weakest point, and—' He shuddered, not wanting to say the dreaded words, bacterial endocarditis. 'Is she taking her iron and folic acid?'

'She has no choice,' smiled Lucy. 'She gets it!'

'When should we start the subcutaneous heparin?'

'Not till thirty-eight weeks. We don't want to thin her blood unnecessarily, Pino.'

'But it's to prevent blood clots forming at the birth!'

'And I'm concerned about preventing haemorrhage at the birth! Let's leave it to d'Arc to decide.'

'But he's not a cardiologist—'

'Maybe not, but he's pretty good on cardiac conditions in obstetrics, as you very well know!' returned Lucy firmly, though she squeezed his hand as she spoke. 'Try not to worry too much, Pino. So often these mothers with heart murmurs have a remarkably quick and easy delivery, as if Nature was compensating them. We'll return her to the maternity unit two weeks before she's due, and they'll keep a close observation on her.'

'She won't want to go and leave Silvio.'

'Pino, *caro mio*, she will have to go, and you will have to be firm with her.'

'Oh, Lucia, I am sorry. You know how it is with our relatives and friends!'

'Yes, Pino, I do—only too well.'

He returned her hand-clasp with a look that melted all her resistance. 'And now tell me about yourself, *amore mio*, and how you are coping with the guests.'

'Let's say that I'm learning to be flexible! No sooner is one problem sorted out than there's another, and no two are ever exactly alike,' she replied, her eyes lighting up with interest.

'For instance, most of the guests can take their medication in tablet form, but if they feel too nauseated I try intramuscular injection if there's enough muscle to avoid bruising. Giving an anti-emetic before the radiotherapy seems to suit some; otherwise a liquid preparation, chased down with a sweet, might be tolerated better. Everybody's different!'

He nodded. 'Yes, we have to—er—make battle with each new problem as it arises!'

'We have to be persistent in finding out the best solution,' she agreed. 'And it's the same with their diet. The food here is excellent but to someone feeling weak and lethargic it has no taste or, worse still, everything tastes horrid. I try to tempt them with fresh fruit juice and fortified high-protein drinks— and, to be honest, I think a glass of wine or a small gin and tonic can be a splendid appetiser, don't you? Moderation in all things—a good motto!'

'Ah, a doctor after the *contessa's* own heart!' he grinned, fascinated by the way her eyes sparkled as she talked about her work. He remembered the warily hesitant English girl he had met at the Venice convention only a month before. What a contrast to the vibrant young woman talking with him now!

'And of course the most important factor of all is the state of mind,' she continued eagerly. 'If fear and anxiety can be removed, tension is relieved and that eases pain and discomfort. And *that* reduces the need for pain-relieving drugs. It means they need to talk their feelings through, and get it all out into the open.

'I always take plenty of time when discussing problems with guests and their relatives—so often it's a listening ear that's needed.'

'Which is quite clearly your special talent, Lucia,' he said admiringly. 'We must take the spiritual needs of our patients into account, along with the physical, especially in a hospice like this, yes?'

'But of course!' replied Lucy, her eyes shining softly. 'And each one is an individual, with his or her own ideas about facing the possibility of death. We have to help them to come to terms with it in their own way. We're back where we started, aren't we? Everybody's different!'

She became conscious of his intense dark gaze, and her colour rose.

'Pino! You are deliberately making me rattle on and on!'

'Ah, Lucia—I could look at you and listen to your voice for hours on end.'

His mention of hours made her look at her watch.

'Heavens, it's nearly six! I only intended to take a few minutes' break, and—'

'*E dopo*—I come along with my listening ear,' he grinned.

'I must not waste any more time,' she said severely, getting up and returning to her duties, but there was a new lightness in her step because Pino Ponti had returned to the Villa Luisa.

Cecilia's preparations for the wedding went ahead rapidly and, in spite of all efforts to keep it quiet, the news got around that the beautiful Gabriella Rasi was to be married in Venice to an eminent doctor.

The actress arrived back at the Villa Luisa that

weekend, and the wedding was planned for the following Wednesday afternoon at the church which had featured in one of her best films, La Pietà on the Riva degli Schiavoni.

It had stood facing the Lagoon since the eighteenth century, when Antonio Vivaldi had attended there and given performances of his latest compositions, and Gabriella had made up her mind to be married to Findlay there.

A splendidly decorated barge was hired to take the wedding party across the Lagoon to the church and return them to the reception at the villa.

Guests who came from a distance were booked in at the Hotel des Deux Lions, and these included Mr and Mrs Henri d'Arc, the groom's parents. Signore and Signora Rasi came from their home at Padua, returning on the same day after seeing their daughter married.

The honeymoon destination was the ancient and sparsely populated island of Torcello, where the couple could enjoy peace and privacy without being too far away if Gabriella needed medical care.

A senior nurse, Marcella, was left in charge of the Villa Luisa for the two hours that the *contessa* and the two doctors were at the wedding, and Pino had his mobile phone.

Lucy wore a tailored dress and jacket in blue, white and violet, topped with a straw hat trimmed with flowers that echoed the tones of her outfit. She and the *contessa* helped the bride to put on a simple white dress that made her look like a Greek goddess, with her golden hair swirled up into a knot clipped with a spray of white roses.

The barge set out in glorious sunshine beneath a cloudless blue sky, the bride reclining beneath a canopy of blue and gold.

It might have been a scene of medieval Venice, thought Lucy as they approached the incomparable Venetian skyline, where St Mark's Square and the Doge's Palace stood at the entrance to the Grand Canal, with the dome of Santa Maria della Salute on the opposite bank. Pino came to her side and lightly touched her shoulder.

'See there, Lucia,' he said, pointing across the expanse of water. '*Il bacino di San Marco*—the old seaport, the basin of St Mark's, yes?'

'Yes, I see it,' she smiled.

'But it is also called *il bacio di San Marco*—the kiss of St Mark's—because there the water comes right up to the edge of the piazza, the place where Venice and the sea have kissed for centuries.'

And he gave a demonstration of *un bacio* beneath the brim of her flowery hat. Lucy caught her breath, and saw Gabriella's smiling nod of approval. Oh, what a charmer he could be!

The party disembarked on the quayside in front of La Pietà, where d'Arc waited with Padre Renato. Gabriella's mother and father supported their daughter on either side as she walked into the church and everybody followed them in, taking their places beneath Tiepolo's magnificent ceiling painting of *The Glories of Paradise*. The ceremony was kept short, but was heart-rendingly moving as the two voices were heard making their solemn vows.

When the newly married couple emerged into the sunshine, to the strains of Vivaldi's 'Primavera', a

spontaneous burst of applause greeted the bride, and
passing strangers stopped to stare as cameras clicked
and confetti was thrown. Any tears were discreetly
wiped away for this was Gabriella's day of joy, with
no place for sad thoughts and future uncertainties.

On arrival back at the villa, Lucy quickly donned
a white coat over her wedding outfit and went to
check on the resident guests. Marcella reported that
they were all comfortable, and added that Vittorio
Goldoni had had a visitor.

'Really? Was it his godfather, *Zio* Faro?'
asked Lucy.

'*Si, Dr Lucia, il Conte di Mirano,*' the nurse
replied.

'What? Did I hear you say *Conte*?' gasped Lucy,
unable to believe her ears.

'I think that the count does not like to be
recognised,' said Marcella slowly. 'I have seen him
on another occasion—that is how I knew his face.
And perhaps, *dottoressa*, it would be wise not to
mention his visit.'

Lucy was sure that the nurse knew more than she
was revealing. There was certainly a mystery of some
kind here, and once again she wondered about this
count's past association with the Countess Favaro—
a love affair that had ended in disappointment?
On Gabriella's wedding day Lucy decided to
follow Marcella's advice and say nothing that might
embarrass Cecilia.

The reception in the garden was now under way,
with smiles and congratulations on all sides. All the
residents were visited by the new Signora d'Arc with
glasses of champagne, and at six o'clock she changed

into a cool, cream, linen two-piece suit and prepared to leave for Torcello. She said goodbye to her parents, in-laws and guests, and gave Lucy a special hug.

'Pino loves you, *cara mia amica*—I tell you that you will be the next bride!' she whispered, echoing Lucy's own secret desires. The bride was now looking tired, and her husband anxiously drew her away to where the wedding barge waited on the inlet used by the ambulances.

'Arrivederci, Gabriella e Findlay—arrivederci!' The farewells sounded across the water as the canopied barge drew away from the land. Gabriella's wedding day was over, and all her friends rejoiced that the man she loved would be at her side for the rest of her life.

Life returned to normal at the villa, and Lucy's workload eased; having Pino back made a difference, and with every day that passed the two doctors grew closer as partners and friends.

Lucy was happy and fulfilled in her work, and at times felt almost certain that Giuseppe Ponti returned her love for him; yet somehow their relationship remained static, with no deepening of commitment on his part.

She noticed that Cecilia sometimes gave her oddly questioning looks, as if she wanted to tell her something but was not at liberty to do so.

One morning, over coffee, Lucy decided to tackle the *contessa* in a roundabout way.

'Dr Ponti is looking happier these days,' she said lightly. 'Do you think he could possibly be in love?'

Cecilia glanced up quickly and chose her words with care.

'How should I know, Lucia? He is very attractive to women, as you have seen, and many have imagined him in love with them—only to be disappointed. No doubt he will settle down in time, but—' She bit her lip, frowned and reluctantly continued.

'My dear Lucia, I would advise caution. There are certain—er—*complicazione*. Forgive me, I must get back to my work!'

It was difficult not to be offended by such an obvious warning off, and Lucy's colour rose. Clearly there were undercurrents of which she was unaware, and she wondered if the *contessa* was obliquely referring to the difference in nationality and background between Ponti and herself.

She was sure in her own mind that the love she felt for Pino could and would overcome any such objections; they were equals in their chosen profession, which surely rose above any class and cultural differences, she reasoned. In her newly found confidence and independence she saw no bar to eventual happiness.

Unless. . . Had Pino really recovered from his earlier love for Gabriella? Was he ready to make a real commitment to another woman—herself? Could she ever hope to take first place in his life? The niggling imp of doubt remained. If only she could be sure!

By the beginning of May Vittorio Goldoni had endured the first four weeks of megavoltage radiotherapy, and felt as if every ounce of vitality had been knocked out of him.

'Even if I survive the disease, Dr Ponti, I am not sure that I shall recover from the treatment,' he joked weakly to Pino and Lucy on his latest return from *radioterapia*.

'Courage, Vittorio, you are doing well,' she told him, offering a sip of iced water. He made a face as the glass touched his lips.

'Ugh! My mouth is sore and my breath must be disgusting,' he groaned, turning away from her.

Lucy sighed, but Pino was alerted. 'Open your mouth, my friend, and let me see,' he ordered, pointing out to a horrified Lucy several small ulcers on the tongue and the inside of the patient's cheeks.

'I cannot clean my teeth, *dottore*, not even with a soft brush. It is too painful,' admitted the young man wearily.

'Why did you not tell me this, Vittorio?' Lucy asked, while inwardly reproaching herself.

'I thought it was just one more thing I had to bear,' he replied, and Lucy felt further shamed for her lack of observation. Pino smiled and nodded understandingly.

'We'll give you an antiseptic mouthwash and a bacteriostatic solution to paint those ulcers, Vittorio,' he promised. 'And now I must go to see my sister. She is complaining of backache, and we do not want her to commence labour too soon!'

With an upward roll of his eyes he left them, and Lucy hurried to bring Vittorio the mouthwash at once.

'If my life is spared, Dr Lucia, I shall be a changed man,' he told her seriously, and she could see that he meant every word. He had told her something of his privileged background and his playboy's existence among the clubs and fashionable bars of Milan and Rome.

'That life is over now, Dr Lucia. I no more want to live for pleasure, but to do good with my life if there is still time. There is nothing like a brush with death to sort out the priorities, yes?'

Lucy was touched by his words, and continued to sit by his side until he fell asleep. As she rose to tiptoe out of the room a nurse came to say that Vittorio's visitor had called again. She asked him to come with her to the back veranda, and told him that his godson could not be disturbed while resting after radiotherapy.

'I understand, Dr Spriggs. Poor Vittorio!'

The count seemed restless and uneasy as he stood gazing out across the sea to the Venetian coastline. Lucy attempted to raise his spirits a little.

'When the treatment is finished he will start feeling better, *signore*. Dr Scogliera says that the survival rate is more than ninety per cent when radiotherapy is begun at Stage I of this condition,' she said with a smile.

He turned abruptly and faced her.

'Does it bother you, Dr Spriggs, that I have come here again?'

She was taken aback. There was something about this man, with his sombre eyes and courtly manners, that intrigued her and she felt that there were unspoken words in the air.

'Why should it bother me, *signore*?' she asked

directly. 'Is there any reason why you should not come to the Villa Luisa?'

'Ah! *Cara dottoressa*, if you only knew. . .' He spoke half under his breath, and could not hide his agitation. He paced up and down the veranda, clenching and unclenching his hands. Lucy began to feel concerned but remained outwardly calm. She sat down in one of the basket chairs and waited.

'Is the Contessa Favaro at home today?' he asked.

'Yes, she is in her office, *signore*. Do you wish to see her?'

'Oh, no, I think not, Dr Spriggs, she may not wish to—to— You say she is well?'

'Very well, and always busy!' smiled Lucy.

'That is good.' He paused. 'And does her—her nephew visit sometimes?'

'Her nephew, *signore*?' Lucy was puzzled. The *contessa* had never referred to any relatives.

'He is a doctor with a practice here on the Lido, I believe,' he said nervously.

Lucy's heart began to beat faster as she took in these words. The mystery was about to be unfolded, she felt. She took a deep breath before replying.

'I did not know that Cecilia—that the *contessa* had a nephew living near,' she said carefully, making an effort to sound matter-of-fact. 'There is a doctor who runs his general practice from here.'

'Here? Here at the Villa Luisa?' He looked startled.

'Yes, *signore*. A Dr Ponti—Giuseppe Ponti.'

There was a stunned silence. He turned and looked at her, his face pale and with an expression that she found difficult to fathom. And it was then that she saw the resemblance.

'*O mio Dio—Giuseppe!*' he murmured, and she heard the deep yearning in the words. She rose, trembling slightly, determined to be of service to this man if she could.

'You know him, then, *signore*?'

'Yes—no, not really—er—I was acquainted with a tutor of his at the University of Padua, where he learned to be a doctor. His results were always so good—so glowing with praise! A brilliant young man, Dr Spriggs—*magnifico*!'

While she pondered on her next move Lucy heard the sound of Pino's feet descending the stairs, and her thoughts raced ahead of her judgement: should she take a gamble on boldness again?

'Please take a seat, *signore*,' she said. 'Wait here for a moment. I will return very soon.'

'Dr Spriggs!' he called after her as she disappeared through the door into the corridor behind the verandah. She did not turn back.

Ponti had reached the bottom of the staircase, and was about to make his way towards the surgery.

'Pino!' she called out.

'*Ciao*, Lucia!'

'Wait! I have someone here to see you.'

He stopped and smiled. 'Gabriella and Findlay?'

'No!'

'Valeria? Gianni? His Holiness the Pope? *Accidenti!* Not your lady mother?'

'No! Come with me, Pino, and be prepared for a great surprise. *Andiamo!*'

He obediently took her outstretched hand and let himself be led to the veranda.

'What is this, Lucia? *Che cos'è?*'

'Wait and see.'

They went onto the veranda, Lucy leading. The Count of Mirano stood facing them, his hands clasped together so tightly that the knuckles showed white.

'There, see!' Lucy's violet-blue eyes shone as she made the formal introduction in her best hostess manner. 'Dr Giuseppe Ponti, allow me to present you to—*il Conte di Mirano*!'

The older man stood absolutely still as if transfixed, a whole series of emotions following in quick succession across his features: joy, hope and fear were all there.

'Giuseppe, mio caro figlio.' My son. My dear son.

Lucy closed her eyes momentarily. Yes, of course. Deep down she had known that this man was Ponti's real father. She turned to see the son's reaction.

What she saw made her recoil in horrified surprise. His face was dark with fury.

'What are you doing here, Favaro?' he demanded harshly in Italian. 'Why do you show your face now after years of disowning me? I am the son of Bruno Ponti, who married the woman you betrayed.'

The count put out a hand, as if warding off a blow. 'If you only knew my regrets, Giuseppe— the remorse I live with daily—you might show me some mercy.'

His voice was only just audible. Lucy went to his side and helped him to sit down. He sank into the wicker chair as if he were mortally wounded.

'What mercy did you show to an innocent servant girl when you turned her out with her unborn child?' asked Ponti with a face like stone. 'A better man rescued her and was not ashamed to call her son his

own. I do not know what tale you have told Dr
Spriggs but I have nothing to say to you, Favaro, and
neither has my aunt Cecilia, who has done more for
me than you ever did.'

The Count buried his head in his hands, and Lucy
put an arm across his bowed shoulders as she
faced Ponti.

'I owe you both an apology for my presumption,'
she said in a voice of ice. 'When Count Favaro came
to visit his godson he spoke so warmly of you, Dr
Ponti, that I made the mistake of thinking that you
would receive him with common courtesy at least.
Clearly I was mistaken.'

'After the way this man treated my mother, Lucia,
I feel nothing for him but contempt,' rasped Ponti,
the anger in his dark eyes making him seem like a
stranger.

'Then be good enough to leave us, please.' Her
own voice took on the upper-class English accent
that had amused him at their first meeting. 'Whatever
the rights and wrongs of the past you've taken your
revenge today, and I hope you're satisfied.'

She patted the count's shoulder, and the sight of
the gesture infuriated Ponti who turned on her, his
eyes blazing with scorn.

'Oh, yes, take pity on him, he's a count, isn't he,
and your mother would be duly impressed! Let me
tell you, Honourable Dr Hallcross-Spriggs, I spit on
all titles that have no meaning! I want no title but
dottore—something I have earned!'

Lucy turned very pale. Favaro rose unsteadily to
his feet, his face grey.

'I provided money for her, Giuseppe; she was

never in want,' he said in a low voice. 'And your fees at Padua—'

'I shall pay back every lira.'

Count Favaro stood up straight and faced his accuser with a certain sorrowful dignity.

'I do not deny the charges you have made against me, Giusep—Dr Ponti, but let me assure you that I have been punished. My marriage was childless and ended in divorce. I wanted to be reconciled with your mother—the only woman I have ever truly loved—but she had her own life with Ponti, and I had to keep away and not see her—or you. I shall not trouble you again. *Molte grazie*, Dr Spriggs. You meant to do good, and it is not your fault that Dr Ponti cannot forgive. *Buongiorno.*'

He walked across the veranda and down the steps. Lucy's heart ached as she watched him go—he seemed to have aged ten years in the past few minutes. This is all my doing, she thought wretchedly; through my arrogant misjudgement I have made matters even worse than they were before. She looked at Ponti and saw no pity in his eyes, only naked pain.

'I feel sorry for you, Pino,' she told him quietly. 'It must be hard to live with an unforgiving spirit. At least I have found out in time.'

'All right, so you have found me out, Lucia! And perhaps it is better this way. You could never understand the pride of a Venetian—the lifelong duty of a man to defend his mother's honour. You think that just because he is the Count of—'

'I don't care who he is. I only see a man who has paid a terrible price for his past mistakes, and yet you kick him when he is down—his own son!' she retorted bitterly. 'I don't want to hear any more, or stay in this place another day—not another hour!'

The tears of disillusionment, which she had managed to hold in check, now spilled over and blinded her as she stumbled from the veranda and made her way up to her room, where she took down her suitcase from the top of the wardrobe.

As she folded her clothes and hastily packed her few belongings there was a knock on the door.

'Lucia, let me in, please.' It was Cecilia.

'Come in, *contessa*, but don't waste your time trying to make me change my mind,' said Lucy tightly. 'After all, you did try to warn me off your nephew.'

'Oh, please do not condemn him for what has happened today, Lucia,' pleaded Cecilia, sitting down on the bed. 'I tried several times to persuade him to tell you about his family history, but he was afraid, I think.'

'What, that I would be impressed to hear that he was the son of a count, even though illegitimate?' asked Lucy bitterly, bustling around the room, emptying the wardrobe and fetching items from the bathroom. 'What an insult! As if I care a fig whether his father's a count or a Venetian boatman! No, I was foolish enough to think that he cared for me, but now I doubt whether he's capable of caring for anyone—'

She choked on the words as she slammed down the top of the case.

'But he has been much hurt, Lucia,' protested the *contessa*, 'so much that he never mentions the Favaros, or calls me aunt. The irony is that he is a Favaro through and through, with their good looks and brains! We can trace our ancestry back to the eleventh century, when Favaros went on the Fourth Crusade and fought with the Genoese—'

'So what? Does that excuse Pino's unforgiving attitude towards the count?' Lucy cut in. 'And what about *you*, Cecilia; you're a Favaro, and you're not hard and cruel!'

'I have their stubbornness, Lucia,' sighed the *contessa*. 'I defied my parents and refused to marry the man they'd chosen for me, and took nursing training instead. I was a sister at the hospital where my nephew was a medical student, and when I decided to spend my inheritance on the Villa Luisa to turn it into a hospice we came to the arrangement that he runs his practice from the villa and we share our finances. Money is always a problem, but Giuseppino helps me out.

'I had drifted away from my brother because of the bad feeling, and—'

She broke off and shook her head regretfully. 'I blame myself, Lucia. I should have made more effort to heal the pain of rejection which has overshadowed Giuseppino's life.'

'I don't see why it's your fault that your nephew can't forgive that poor, lonely man who has been so kind to his godson, Cecilia,' retorted Lucy. 'And I *can't* stay here after what I heard and saw this afternoon. I'm terribly sorry to walk out on you and the guests, but you managed without me before and you must manage again. I have been mistaken in Dr Ponti!'

'But Lucia, *cara mia*—'

'No, Cecilia, I don't belong here.' Lucy's tone was

final. 'It's not the first time that I've behaved foolishly with a man I thought was in love with me, but
this time I'm not going to mope around in self-pity.
Dr Ponti has plenty of superficial charm but he seems
to be incapable of loving anybody—and that goes for
all the women who fling themselves at him, myself
included, you'll say!'

'Lucia! I say no such thing. Please let me—'

'No, Cecilia, there's nothing more to be said. I
count myself fortunate that I've found out the truth
about him sooner rather than later. Will you call a
taxi for me, please?'

There were tears in both women's eyes when the
moment came for parting. They embraced before
Lucy got into the taxi and headed for the landing-
point at Santa Maria Elizabetta.

On the familiar journey across the Lagoon Lucy
stood at the rail of the *vaporetto*, watching the Lido
recede. Another water-bus took her up the Grand
Canal to the Piazza Roma, where a further taxi carried
her to Marco Polo Airport.

Rather than wait for the next flight to Heathrow,
she boarded a flight leaving almost at once for
Amsterdam where, after a two-hour wait, she got a
seat on a plane going to Heathrow, using her Visa
card. She went through the various customs and pass-
port controls like an automaton, boarding and leaving
the aircraft as if in a dream—not daring to relax her
rigid self-control for an instant.

It was getting towards dusk by the time she arrived
at Heathrow and boarded the airport bus for central
London. By now she felt too exhausted to face the
train journey from Waterloo Station down to

Wiltshire and Hallcross Park. Besides, her parents were not expecting her, and she felt that her father should not be disturbed at such a late hour.

She hailed a taxi and gave the address of the flat Sir Peter used when he had to stay overnight at the Ministry, and where she had often stayed during her training at St Margaret's Hospital.

'Why, Dr Spriggs! I heard you were in Italy for six months,' said the woman caretaker when Lucy rang her doorbell. 'Your father will be so pleased to see you home again!'

And it was at that moment that Lucy knew that there could be no going back to her former life, over-protected to the point of suffocation by her doting parents. Right now all she needed was a night's rest, and from tomorrow she would have to start organising her new, independent life away from Hallcross Park.

And away from the Villa Luisa. For ever.

CHAPTER EIGHT

Sir Peter and Lady Hallcross-Spriggs were overjoyed at hearing from Lucy that she had left Italy,
but their relief turned to bewildered disappointment
when they realised that she did not intend to return
to Hallcross Park.

'If I could use your flat for a while, Daddy, I need
to find a job in London,' she explained on
the telephone. 'I'm a doctor, and I want to go on
practising.'

Immediately after her return she had applied for a
resident medical officer's post in a north London
hospice, but there were currently no vacancies. In
fact, the only work she had been able to obtain was
as a junior doctor in the accident and emergency
department of a somewhat run-down hospital in an
area notorious for crime and drugs.

It was far from easy and, particularly on the night
shifts, she encountered some fairly rough characters,
frequently accompanied by police officers who gave
her sympathetic looks and adopted a protective attitude towards her.

However, they soon found that pretty young Dr
Spriggs could vigorously stand up for victims of viol-
ence and abuse, while leering louts wilted beneath
her flashing violet-blue eyes. The work was both
exhausting and emotionally draining, but it was a

challenge and helped her to forget her lost paradise
across the Lagoon. . .

By the last week in May, when Lucy had resisted all
her parents' attempts to persuade her to come home,
Lady Philippa travelled up to London to try to reason
with her over a restaurant lunch.

'Thank heaven you came to your senses in time
over that Dr Ponti, Lucinda!' she sighed. 'I mean,
just think of his background—that impossible sister
and brother-in-law!'

'As a matter of fact, Mummy, the Pontis are only
half his family.' Lucy simply could not resist
revealing Ponti's true parentage, if only to see her
mother's reaction.

'A *count*, Lucinda? Count Favaro of Mirano? Good
heavens! Well, that explains why he looks so unlike
that Capogna creature. And so he's the countess's
nephew—well! Whoever would have thought it?
When did he tell you all this?'

But Lucy was not inclined to go into details of the
revelation that had shattered her happiness and driven
her from the Villa Luisa. All she wanted was to forget
that hateful scene on the veranda which had ended
her foolish dreams.

Yet it was in her dreams at night that the happy
scenes came back to her. She would see again the
shimmering waters of the Lagoon and 'the kiss of St
Mark's'; Gabriella's lovely face as she sailed to her
wedding. Lucy—*Lucia*—would be back among the
guests at the villa, reasoning with Maria and encouraging Vittorio. When she woke up and found herself
in Sir Peter's flat there was a yearning sense of

loss as the pictures faded from her mind.

One morning a letter arrived in a long crested envelope, sent on from Hallcross Park, and Lucy held her breath as she tore it open. It was from the count, and after thanking her for caring so well for Vittorio Goldoni—now happily restored to his family and feeling better every day—Favaro went on to apologise for the fiasco that had resulted from her attempt to introduce him to his own son.

'It was not your fault, Dr Spriggs, and I thank you for your goodwill,' he wrote in careful English. 'I have since had conversation with my sister, the Countess Favaro, and I have learned that there was a close attachment between Dr Ponti and yourself, now sadly broken. How can I express my regret? With what a full heart, dear Dr Spriggs, would I have received you as my daughter. . .'

Lucy could read no more, and hid the letter in a drawer. Oh, how could she have been so foolishly impulsive? Yet she would have had to learn the truth some time, not only about Ponti's history but his inability to forgive the past actions of a man who now so desperately longed for reconciliation.

As it was, she had found out in time to save herself later disillusionment over this hard, unrelenting aspect of Ponti's character, to say nothing of his unwillingness to commit himself to a serious relationship. Had she made her own feelings for him too obvious? Anyway, it made no difference now!

Her father took the opportunity to visit her at the flat whenever he could. One surprising piece of news he told her was that Aubrey Portwood was now seeing Meg Elstone on a fairly regular basis. Lucy was at first taken aback, but on reflection realised that she had done Meg a favour.

'It explains such a lot,' she pointed out. *'That's* why she had such funny moods, and was so cool towards me—she wanted him for herself! Well, in many ways it's a good match, and I'm happy for them both, aren't you, Daddy?'

'Are you really happy, darling?' countered Sir Peter with sadness in his eyes. 'You've lost weight, and sometimes you look so—so far away.'

'Don't worry about me, Daddy, I'm fine.'

What else could she say? She could hardly weep upon his shoulder and tell him everything in her heart, for he was still convalescing from a serious illness brought on by her own wilful behaviour; she must not give him any further anxiety.

But Sir Peter was by no means convinced.

Lucy had two days off, but had woken early. She lay listening to the roar of traffic in the street below, and wondered if this would be a good opportunity to visit Hallcross Park at last. The rhododendrons would be in bloom at this prettiest time of the year, and she was longing for some country air.

The sudden intrusion of the telephone on her reflections made her start; it was not yet seven. Who could be calling at this hour? She reached out to pick up the extension.

'Hello?'

'Lucia! Buongiorno—sono Cecilia Favaro.'

'Oh!'

Lucy lay back on the pillow, holding the receiver to her ear with a shaking hand. The *contessa's* voice brought back in an instant the sights, the sounds and the very smells of the Villa Luisa as vividly as if Lucy were there.

'I telephoned your home, and your father gave me this number, Lucia. I am very sorry to disturb you, *cara mia*,' said the *contessa* gravely, 'but I must tell you that Gabriella d'Arc is back with us. She was taken ill on Torcello, and her condition is now much worse. In fact, I fear that she must soon leave us. Findlay has sent for her parents and his own—'

'Oh, no!' breathed Lucy. 'And we so hoped for a miracle—poor Findlay.'

'Listen, Lucia, she is asking for you. Hour after hour she asks, *''Dov'è Lucia?''* She wants very much to see you.'

'But, Cecilia, I can't come back—I can't! I have commitments here now!' Lucy cried distractedly, sitting up and gesturing with her hands as if the *contessa* could see her.

'Then I must tell Gabriella that you send your love to her, and that you are happy,' said Cecilia sadly. 'Forgive me, Lucia, but I did promise her that I would speak to you.'

'Oh, what shall I do?' wailed Lucy, clutching at her forehead in dismay. 'Cecilia, wait, listen—I will come over—today, just to see her, but I must return tomorrow because—'

'*Va bene! Molte grazie, Lucia, molte grazie*—I will tell her that you come today, yes?'

'*Va bene, Cecilia. Arrivederci!*'

She replaced the handset and lifted it again to dial Heathrow International Airport. She also telephoned Hallcross Park, praying that her father would answer,

which he did. When she told him that she was flying
out to Venice he was worried but understanding.

'Go and do what you have to do, darling, and keep
in touch with us. We'll be waiting for you. Please
give d'Arc my condolences—that was a damned
good paper of his at the convention. Sad business
about his poor little wife. Take care, Lucinda.'

His words were a comfort to Lucy on the airport
bus to Heathrow, and during the flight across Europe.
When the taxi from Marco Polo Airport brought her
to the Piazza Roma and the waiting *vaporetti* her
heart leapt to see the Grand Canal again and the
palaces lining each bank as she was carried along its
length, down to the 'kiss of St Mark's' and the
Lagoon sparkling in the sunshine.

She stood at the rail on the last lap of the journey
over to the Lido, and when the short taxi ride brought
her to the Villa Luisa she was half-afraid to ascend
the familiar stone steps. Would *he* be there? And
what would they say to each other?

Cecilia greeted her with a warm embrace. She
looked tired, and there was a troubled atmosphere
throughout the villa. Unsmiling staff hurried to and
fro, doors slammed and a woman's voice could be
heard loudly sobbing.

'Come to Gabriella now, Lucia—she waits for you
ever since I said you are coming. Padre Renato has
just finished giving her the Sacrament.'

The joyous smile which illumined Gabriella's face
was more than compensation for the upheavals of the
day. Still delicately beautiful as her strength ebbed
away, she was only able to whisper her greeting.

'Thank you for coming back to him, Lucia, *cara amica*. He has need of you.'

'Gabriella. . .'

It was no time for speeches. D'Arc rose and gave Lucy his chair; she sat down beside the bed and silently conveyed her gratitude for all that their brief friendship had meant—right from the moment of their first meeting and the instant rapport they had both felt.

'Now it is time to say goodbye, Lucia.'

The calm blue eyes closed as Gabriella drifted in and out of sleep. When Lucy left the bedside she told d'Arc that she would return to share the watching during the night.

'I have put you in a small room on the third floor,' the *contessa* told her apologetically. 'I have the Rasi parents here, and the d'Arcs—and, most unfortunately, Maria Capogna who has been allowed out of hospital to visit Gabriella. She must have driven the staff mad in the antenatal ward, and the cardiologist gave in and let her out until tomorrow morning.

'It was she who was crying when you arrived because Findlay would not let her weep and wail over Gabriella! She and Silvio are in the room I would have given you—perhaps you will have a word with her, Lucia, as she listens to you. But first you must freshen up after your journey, and then come to have your supper with me.'

It was on the way to Cecilia's room that Lucy encountered Ponti in the corridor. In the subdued light she thought for one moment that he was the Count of Mirano. He looked years older, and there were dark shadows under his eyes. His mouth was a tense, straight line and Lucy felt that she could be looking at the Dr Ponti of the future, a man in middle life haunted by an unresolved sorrow—the loss of the woman he had once loved.

A man like the Count of Mirano.

'Lucia! It was good of you to come.' He held out his hand, and when she touched it he seized hers and gripped it tightly.

'How could I refuse when the *contessa* telephoned me this morning?' she asked, thankful that he could not guess her inner confusion. 'Oh, here's Briciola,' she added, as Gabriella's cat purred around her legs in welcome. She withdrew her hand and bent down to pick up the animal, which nuzzled against her neck.

'Gabriella kept asking for you, Lucia, and Cecilia felt that she should—'

'Yes, of course.' She stroked the cat's ears with a slightly unsteady hand, aware that Ponti's agitation matched her own.

'Your father, Lucia—is he keeping well now?'

'Thank you, yes. He has returned to part-time work.'

There was a pause, and she said awkwardly, 'This is a very hard time for you all, Pino.'

'Yes, and most of all for Findlay. We have to keep going,' he replied with a heavy sigh. 'And you, Lucia? You are happy to be with your own people again?'

'Thank you, yes. I—I'm working in London.'

She glanced up at him and saw the intensity of his gaze. They might have stood there for ever, she felt, had she not made her excuses, saying that the *contessa* expected her.

Over supper Lucy was aware of tension.

'You look worn out, Cecilia. Do let me help while I'm here,' she said, brushing aside her own weariness. 'You've had a lot of extra work, with Gabriella and her relatives here.'

The *contessa* shook her head. 'Not at all, Lucia. I am used to this kind of nursing, and dealing with distressed families. No, it is the—er—*desolazione* in Giuseppino's eyes that makes me unhappy. We are all touched by Gabriella's tragedy and our hearts ache for Findlay, but it is since you went away, Lucia, that Giuseppino has been so miserable.

'All his teasing ways have gone; he does not speak; he does not smile, except with his patients and to comfort Findlay. And he takes no pleasure in anything. He looks—well, you have seen how he looks, Lucia.'

Lucy stared into the *contessa's* troubled eyes, and could think of nothing to say. Could her absence have made so much difference?

'*Contessa*, I am very sorry,' she sighed at last. 'You know the reason why I went away. You warned me yourself that Pino was attractive to women, but that he'd been unable to settle with any one woman since he lost Gabriella to d'Arc. And then, when that terrible scene with his father took place, I could not stand it any longer, as you saw.'

'Yes, Lucia, but I was wrong!' cried Cecilia despairingly. 'Since you left I have seen how much his heart now longs for you! Tell me, if there was a—a *riconciliazione* between my brother and my nephew, would that change your feelings at all?'

Lucy hesitated under the *contessa's* intent gaze.

She struggled inwardly with her confused thoughts, her commitments, her responsibilities, her secret desires.

'I have chosen to return to my life in England, Cecilia,' she said at last. 'We all learn from our experiences, and I learned a lot during my time here. But things have changed, and now—'

She looked straight at the *contessa*. 'And I do not believe that your nephew will ever be reconciled to his father.'

The *contessa* leaned back in her chair and closed her eyes.

'*Capisco*. I understand. There is nothing more to be said.'

Lucy had to be very firm with Maria Capogna, who was hanging around outside Gabriella's door.

'You are to go straight to bed, Maria, and I will bring you a warm drink,' she told the girl. 'Tomorrow morning, if Mr d'Arc allows you in, you may see her before you return to the hospital, which is where you should be now.'

She steeled herself against Maria's tearful protests, and beckoned to the unhappy Silvio, who had borne the brunt of his wife's complaints about the treatment she had received and her inconsolable grief over *la belle Signora d'Arc*.

'You are to see that she stays in her room, Silvio, or there will be trouble. The staff are very busy, and there are many in need of comfort. Maria must be brave, and pray for Gabriella and her family. No, I do not want to hear another word, Maria. Not another sound, do you understand?'

Silvio put his arm around his wife's bulging frame and led her away to their room, promising Lucy that there would be no more demands from her that day.

Or rather that night, for it was now nearly ten. When two nurses came to Gabriella's room with clean linen and all the requirements for general nursing care, Findlay emerged with his weary-eyed parents and in-laws and Lucy begged them to take a rest while she sat beside the bed for a couple of hours. Tired as she was, she welcomed the chance of a vigil alone with her friend.

'Of course I'll call you if I think you should come, Findlay,' she assured him. 'Only do try to persuade her parents to go to bed. They look exhausted.'

He gripped her shoulder in wordless gratitude, and when the nurses had finished their task Lucy took her place beside the newly made bed. The room was filled with the fragrance of Gabriella's favourite perfume and she was sleeping on her side, one pale hand on the bed-cover. Lucy leaned back in the chair and let her limbs relax, while her thoughts wandered back over the long day. Her eyes closed.

A light sound made her open her eyes and sit up sharply. Giuseppe Ponti was seated on the other side of the bed. He had tiptoed into the room while Lucy dozed, and now he was putting his finger to his lips as he regarded her. She gave him a half-smile, and they both looked towards the girl in the bed between them.

Lucy wondered if Pino's thoughts were the same as her own. Gabriella was thirty-one years old, but how much she had achieved in her life! A successful career as an actress, marriage to a man who adored

her, many friendships and no enmities—for even her
screen rivals were friends. Her beauty was unsullied
by any excesses or harmful addictions; fame had not
spoiled her sunny, loving disposition. It was a life to
rejoice over and give thanks for, even though it was
ending so early.

She caught Pino's eye, and was certain that he
shared her reflections. She thought of his father,
whose life had been blighted by a loveless marriage,
loneliness and estrangement from his only child. How
much happier this girl had been!

Gabriella stirred and surfaced from her peaceful
sleep. When she saw their faces she gave them a
sweet smile of recognition and sighed with pure con-
tentment.

'*I miei cari amici, Pino e Lucia.*' My dear friends.

Tears sprang to Lucy's eyes but she blinked them
away, and put out a hand to touch Gabriella's as it
lay on the bedspread. Pino did the same, and their
fingers touched and entwined over hers; they both
leaned forward to catch her whispered words.

'*L'amore è il dono pui grande nel mondo.*'

It was her farewell message for them, and she did
not speak again. They sat in silence, pondering the
words—Love is the greatest gift in the world. It was
almost midnight when Findlay returned to take over
the watch.

Lucy silently withdrew ahead of Ponti, and made
her way to the room she had been given. She quickly
undressed and collapsed into the bed, her head aching
and her overwrought brain filled with confused
images of Pino, Gabriella and the count. For a while
she stared up into the semi-darkness of the room, but

fatigue overcame her and she fell into a troubled slumber.

A breeze stirred the curtains and a half-moon rode across the night sky over the dark Adriatic, which rose and fell upon the shingle in a constant low murmur. Within the villa doors opened and closed, a guest's call-bell rang and footsteps were heard. Low voices spoke, stairs creaked, the lift clattered and a distant telephone rang, followed by more footsteps and the sound of Ponti's car departing. Then Lucy became conscious of a persistent knocking that seemed to go on and on; she turned over and finally awoke with a cry. There was somebody at the door of her room.

'*Chi viene?* Who's there?' she called out.

The door opened as she switched on her bedside lamp, and there before her in his nightshirt stood Silvio Capogna.

Lucy blinked and sat up, pulling the duvet around her.

'*Che cosa fa qui?*' she demanded. What are you doing here?

'*Mi dispiace, Dr Lucia,*' he replied in his thick Venetian accent. 'You told my Maria not to make any more noise, but she cannot keep quiet. She is in much pain, *dottoressa*—please, you must come to her!'

Oh, my God, thought Lucy as she took in what he was saying. Oh, no. Let it not be, please—not at this time of all times.

Aloud she said, 'All right, Silvio, don't worry. I will come to her at once. Is there a nurse around? We may need to send for an ambulance to take her to the Ospedale Al Mare, *pronto*!'

She leapt out of bed and threw on her dressing-gown, pushing her feet into the slip-on shoes she had kicked off. She followed Silvio down to the room where Maria lay groaning helplessly in the bed she shared with Silvio.

'Dr Lucia, for two hours I have been in pain!'

'Don't worry, Maria, dear. I'm here to look after you now, and everything is going to be all right,' soothed Lucy with a cheerful air that reassured the Capognas, if not herself.

She turned back the bedclothes. 'Silvio, will you please go and wake the *contessa* and tell her to come at once?'

'*Si, dottoressa, pronto, pronto!*' he muttered.

'Now, Maria, I am just going to have a look down here to see if there is any sign of—'

When Lucy saw the bulging between Maria's sturdy legs she realised that the second stage of labour had begun, and that the baby was advancing through the fully dilated cervix. She glanced round the room and pulled the call-bell.

Maria groaned again as her abdomen hardened with another strong uterine contraction, and before Lucy's eyes appeared the dark circle of the crown of the baby's head.

'Good girl, Maria, take deep breaths in and out like this—and don't push. *Non spingere!*'

She felt Maria's pulse, which was fairly rapid, and checked over in her mind the rules for delivering a woman with a heart condition.

Sit her up on pillows: Maria had three already. Give plenty of pain-relieving sedation: too late now, but Maria was clearly having a quick and easy labour. No pushing: this baby would not need any hard effort on the mother's part. Perform an episiotomy to ease and hasten the birth of the head: no episiotomy scissors, and no time anyway. Give oxygen if the patient goes into heart failure. . .

Cecilia appeared at the door in her dressing-gown, carrying a packet of sanitary pads, another of incontinence pads, a pair of sterile gloves, pre-packed sterile scissors, a dressing-pack and clean bath-towels

'Have we got a cot?' asked Lucy.

'*O mamma mia!*' muttered the *contessa*. 'In the attic!'

'Can Silvio fetch an oxygen cylinder up from the store-room?'

'Yes—shall I ring for an ambulance?'

'No time. Did I hear Pino going out on a call?'

'Yes, about half an hour ago. Do you need Findlay? He's with Gabriella.'

'Let's do this together, Cecilia,' said Lucy steadily. 'We can ask for Findlay if we need him.'

She was now in complete control of the situation, though she was never to forget the next fifteen minutes. She and her assistant had only just time to slip a couple of incontinence pads under Maria's bottom before there was a gush of cloudy fluid and rapid advance of the baby's head.

Nature was merciful, and the birth of Giacomo Capogna was remarkably quick and easy for a first baby. Lucy had only pulled on one glove when she had to steady the head as he was born, and immediately afterwards the body slithered out into her waiting hands. She laid him on a towel and he immediately gasped, opened his mouth and let out an indignant roar at his first encounter with air and light.

Silvio trundled in with the portable oxygen cylinder, and saw his son.

'E' nostro bambino, Maria! Ed è un figlio!' he cried in awe.

Maria leaned forward to see the baby, her broad face now wreathed in smiles, all her pain forgotten in the triumphant joy of motherhood.

'Ciao, Giacomo! Ti chiami Giacomo, mio tesoro!'

Cecilia breathed a prayer of thanks to the Blessed Virgin, and kissed Lucy's cheek in heartfelt gratitude. Lucy felt reasonably satisfied with the mother and baby. Maria was panting but not distressed; in fact, she kept up a voluble recital of endearments and praise of her baby, whose lusty yells were music to Lucy's ears.

She severed and clamped his umbilical cord, wrapped him in a clean towel and handed him to his mother. She judged him to weigh about three point five kilograms, or seven and a half pounds. All his baby-clothes were at the hospital maternity unit, to which he would be transferred with his mother as soon as possible.

The blood loss following the delivery was rather heavy, and Lucy was concerned in case it continued. However, it eased off after the expulsion of the placenta, and an examination showed that no stitches would be needed.

'Will she be able to feed him herself?' asked Cecilia, and while Lucy was explaining that breast-feeding was not usually contra-indicated in mothers with mitral stenosis Maria was busily offering her ample right breast to her son, who needed no encouragement to suck greedily at the nipple.

Lucy had to smile at the ease and naturalness with which the young mother set about her maternal duty, and decided not to make an issue of the delay in reporting the onset of labour, serious though it could have been. The danger was past and, in any case, she was inclined to blame herself for poor Maria's efforts not to make a noise!

In the ensuing silence they heard the sound of Ponti's car returning, and at the same time a murmuring of voices from the floor below. Cecilia gave Lucy a significant look.

'I think Findlay has called the parents, *cara mia*. I will see if he has need of me.'

The sky was brightening, and Lucy went to the window and drew back the curtains upon the sunrise. From the east a shining highway of light stretched across the sea to where the orb of the sun had just appeared over the horizon.

As Lucy drank in the beauty of sky and sea she noticed a white bird flying away over the water, dipping and rising above the pathway of light. As she watched it spread its wings and soared up higher and ever higher until it vanished into the brightness of morning.

She turned back from the window. Maria and Silvio were totally preoccupied with Giacomo, and did not hear the approaching footsteps that stopped at the door. Lucy opened it, and the tall figure of Giuseppe Ponti stood on the threshold. His dark eyes were caverns in the pallor of his face, and Lucy knew what he had come to tell.

'Gabriella è partita.'

She reached out and took his cold hand in hers.

'Yes, Pino. A soul has left this house, and a new life has arrived. Come and see.'

She drew back the door and beckoned him in. He stood as still as a statue, gazing in disbelief at the idyllic scene which met his eyes: the mother and father adoring their baby as he fed from the breast.

'Yes, *Zio* Pino, you are an uncle,' said Lucy softly.

'I—I heard that you were with my sister, Lucia,' he managed to say at last. 'But when? How? Why did you not send for me? Or Findlay?'

'There was very little time to prepare for Giacomo's arrival, it was all so quick and easy,' she told him, adding with a smile, 'I have had six months' recent experience of obstetrics, you know, and Cecilia was a very capable assistant!'

He did not reply, but she saw his dawning smile as Maria looked up and greeted her half-brother. The baby's mouth slipped off the nipple, and she held him upright for his uncle to admire.

The relief and thankfulness on Pino's face as he reached out to take his nephew in his arms was a moving sight to Lucy. He lowered his dark head to kiss the baby's forehead, and she saw how gently, how reverently he held the little body against his heart.

'*O Lucia! O mia cara Lucia!* Shall we ever forget this night?' he whispered, and she saw his mouth soften and quiver. He turned his head aside to hide the emotion which was now beginning to overwhelm him, and Lucy carefully took Giacomo from him to hand back to Maria. Then, putting a firm hand on

Ponti's shoulder, she led him out of the room so that the Capognas would not see his tears or hear the stifled sobs that shook his frame.

'Here, Pino, come with me,' she murmured, and ushered him towards the *contessa's* office, closing the door behind them. She took hold of his hand and he immediately seized hers, kissing it passionately on the palm and on the back. She held him close, and let the flood-tide pour out in a healing stream.

'God forgive me, Lucia, I've been a fool—a proud, misguided fool!' he confessed brokenly. 'That little baby that you have safely brought into the world— he is my nephew, and already I love him. How much more must a man love his own son—oh, Lucia, think of all those years!'

Once again Lucy experienced a sense of destiny unfolding. She began to understand the reason for this tremendous release of pent-up emotion. But now she had learned discretion, and knew that he must find his own way towards reconciliation.

'Pino, *caro mio*, you are overtired and need to rest,' she said, gently withdrawing her arms from around his shoulders. 'This has been a very long night and—'

'Yes, and it is not over yet, Lucia,' he said, straightening himself up and brushing the back of his hand across his eyes. 'I have to make a phone call, and you must be beside me when I make it!'

She indicated the telephone on the desk. 'Do you know the number?' she asked.

'*O mio Dio!* No!'

She opened a top drawer in the desk, and took out a leather-bound address book she she had seen the *contessa* use. He seized it and turned the pages urgently.

'*E' qui*—here it is—' He dialled the number and they waited for what seemed like an eternity. Lucy glanced up at the wall clock. It was not yet five-thirty.

He gave a start and gripped the handset: the call was being answered.

'Favaro? *Il Conte di Mirano?*' he asked breathlessly, and when he heard the assent his voice almost failed.

'*O mio padre—mio caro padre!*'

Lucy made a move to leave the room, but he put out a hand and held her firmly. An incoherent flood of words ended the silence of years. She heard him say, '*Perdonami, ti prego,*' and her own tears flowed as mutual forgiveness was asked and granted. In those few moments the pain of rejection and resentment was swept away for ever, to be replaced by a deep healing and freedom from the shadows of the past.

He then told his father about the passing of Gabriella.

'Yes, father, it was dear Gabriella who brought Lucia back to the Villa Luisa—yes, she is here, father. Lucia, *la donna che amo*, here beside me—and you will never believe what she has done! No, no, something very practical and wonderful—she has delivered my sister Maria of a little son! Yes, a nephew for me—Giacomo!'

Lucy closed her eyes. Laughter and tears, joy and sorrow, life and death—the daily scenes of a doctor's life. And had she really heard those words—'Lucia, the woman I love'?

What should she do? Where did her duty now lie?

She had promised her father that she would return to England today, and she was due back at work in the accident and emergency department tomorrow.

What was she to do? Return to England? Or should she telephone her father and say that she needed to stay at the Villa Luisa for a longer period? She felt that Sir Peter would understand, and want her the best outcome for her.

What should she do?

As she pondered over her dilemma Pino went on talking to his father.

'No, father, no, of course not!' she heard him declare in forceful Italian words. 'I shall *never* let her go again! I nearly went out of my mind while she was away, and it changed everything. I could not bear to lose her, father. No! Yes! You will have your beautiful daughter-in-law, I promise—yes, that *is* what I said, father—you heard me!'

And Lucy heard too. When he finally replaced the receiver and turned to face her, there was no need for questions or answers—no need for words at all as he enfolded her in his arms. Standing in the light that streamed in through the windows of a house that had seen both mourning and rejoicing at dawn, Dr Lucia knew that she had come home for good.

CHAPTER NINE

A WEDDING in Venice at the height of the tourist season is sure to attract attention, especially at a church as prominent as Santa Maria della Salute whose gleaming white marble dome dominates the mouth of the Grand Canal opposite San Marco.

Lucia felt that she owed it to her parents to make the wedding a truly memorable occasion, and the banqueting suite at the Hotel des Deux Lions was booked for the lunch and reception after the ceremony. Two canopied barges were hired to take the wedding party from the Lido to Venice and bring them back.

Pino was irked by the delay. 'Two months to wait until I claim you as my wife!' But Lucia insisted upon a respectful interval after Gabriella's death, and also to allow her parents time to readjust after the shock they had received. Following the events of that unforgettable night of her return to the Villa Luisa, she felt that a period of respite and recovery was needed.

But the weeks had flown by, and the wedding day was almost upon them. Sir Peter and Lady Hallcross-Spriggs arrived the day before, and were booked in at the Hotel des Deux Lions. The Contessa Favaro gave a dinner that evening for them, and also invited Count Favaro and the Goldonis who had travelled down from Milan.

The party was a little stiff and formal at first, although the *contessa* was at her most charming, and drinks were handed round as the guests sat or stood in the main lounge of the Villa Luisa. Sir Peter immediately took to Favaro and old Signore Goldoni, and they were soon chatting happily.

Lady Philippa sat in an aloof silence, barely speaking to her daughter or responding to the *contessa's* eager anticipation of the wedding at eleven the next day.

'St Mary of Health—a very good name for the church, yes? It was built in the seventeenth century in thanksgiving for the end of a great plague,' she told Lady Philippa. 'And we have much to give thanks for today!

'You see young Signore Goldoni over there? He is recovering from a very serious illness, and his parents have shown their gratitude with a magnificent donation. Is not that a blessing, Lady Philippa? I shall have no more financial worries, and will be able to take on more trained staff to care for my guests and—er—*rimettere a nuovo*—refurbish and redecorate the villa.'

'Indeed? I congratulate you,' replied Lady Philippa coldly.

'Yes, isn't it wonderful, Mummy?' cut in Lucia. 'It is to be called L'Ospizio Luisa, and I'm sure it will become a model hospice. We are going to have our own water-ambulance to take guests across the Lagoon, and new equipment and comforts for them. But it will always retain its family atmosphere—'

'Because it is a family business,' smiled the

contessa. 'And how much do we welcome our new member!'

'I'm sure you do.' Lady Philippa did not smile, and Cecilia shrugged helplessly at Lucia.

Pino was then inspired to ask the count to come over and be introduced to Lucia's mother. Favaro bowed politely and kissed her hand, before asking permission to sit down beside her. The *contessa* withdrew, giving Lucia a nod to do likewise.

Lucia was delighted to meet Vittorio again. Although still somewhat underweight and easily tired, he was enormously improved in health and there was a new, purposeful light in his eyes. Although he had managed to keep his illness out of the limelight, his recovery was receiving much attention in headlines like GOLDONI'S SON VISITS NEW CANCER UNIT and DIVA HEIR TO HEAD AIDS RESEARCH CAMPAIGN.

His former friends and associates were baffled by the change in the one-time playboy's lifestyle, and the gossip columns had noted his absence from the nightclub scene as he became increasingly involved with good causes. The Goldonis were honoured guests at the wedding, following their extremely generous gift, and they also shared Favaro's joy in being reunited with his son. Padre Renato summed up the general feeling:

'Only think, Vittorio, if you had not been ill and not come to the Villa Luisa, there might not be this rejoicing today! How often do we see good come out of what seems like disaster?'

Lucia heard his words, and thought how close she had come to losing Pino for ever. She looked across the room to where he stood laughing with the count, though she was too far away to hear what they were saying.

In fact, the count had succeeded where everybody else had failed, and by his adroit flattery of Lady Philippa had thawed out her determination to disapprove of her daughter's marriage. He told her how much he adored his future daughter-in-law, and complimented the mother's beauty and charm, so amazingly duplicated in *cara* Lucia.

'Only I cannot believe that a woman as young as yourself has a daughter old enough to be a doctor,' he added artfully. 'If I had been asked to guess your relation to her I would say sister, *naturalmente*.'

Such compliments, such courtliness as this from the Count of Mirano, eventually broke down Lady Philippa's resistance, and she decided that there would be nothing to lose and a great deal to gain by accepting the inevitable. She gave Favaro her most gracious smile, and he begged to be allowed to escort her in to dinner.

'You seem to have made a hit with Lucia's lady mother,' grinned Pino when Lady Philippa had been called upon to meet Signora Goldoni.

'Ah, yes, Giuseppe, but it has nearly killed me,' answered Favaro with a melodramatic groan. 'Give me a brandy, *mio figlio*; I have done more than my duty for your sake!'

Lucia, out of earshot, smiled in satisfaction at their roar of laughter, and thought what a happy camaraderie there was between them now. . .

Her own father left her in no doubt of his good wishes.

'I knew you weren't happy when you came back in such a hurry, darling, but I can see that everything's all right now. I just wish you weren't so far away,' he said with a sigh.

'You and Mummy will have to come and stay with us, Daddy,' she consoled him. 'After all, it won't be so long now before you retire from politics.'

He nodded fondly. 'Oh, did I tell you that Aubrey and little Miss Elstone have announced their engagement? I think she may be the best person to bolster his ego again, for you know he was terribly disappointed over you, Lucinda.'

Lucia smiled, happy to know that Aubrey's broken heart had been so easily mended. He had sent an original oil painting of an English rural scene as a wedding present, which was very kind of him in the circumstances. Her parents' gift was a pair of splendid Axminster carpets for the home which she and Pino were hoping to purchase close to L'Ospizio Luisa.

'And how's that poor chap, Findlay d'Arc?' inquired Sir Peter.

Lucia shook her head sadly. 'He left for Paris immediately after the funeral, and Pino's had a letter from him to say that he has gone out to Brazil,' she replied. 'He says he no longer has any interest in furthering his career, but wants to work as a doctor on a remote mission station serving the local people.'

'But what a waste of his knowledge and skill!' objected the baronet.

'There'll be plenty of poor patients who'll benefit from his experience, Daddy,' she pointed out, remem-

bering Vittorio's words about his priorities being
changed by an encounter with death.

In spite of a notice put up outside the church to warn
visitors of a service in progress, the sight of the bride
arriving in her barge drew a large number of sight-
seers to the Salute. Tourists and hikers of many
nationalities gathered on the wide flight of marble
steps to see the tall, willowy figure of the bride in
white Burano lace as she went in on her father's arm.

She was attended by Valeria Corsini in a pale green
silk gown with a scooped neckline and wide sleeves
inspired by medieval princesses. It was noted that Dr
Scogliera could not take his eyes from her.

Inside the church everybody rose—everybody,
that is, except Signora Capogna, who sat happily
breast-feeding her rapidly growing baby, Giacomo.
Lady Philippa shuddered at the sight, but Lucia had
a very special smile for Signore Bruno Ponti and his
family who sat together in a group, quite over-
whelmed by the fine company that had come to see
their clever Pino married to his English *dottoressa*.

The ceremony proceeded, with Padre Renato
assisting the celebrant at the Nuptial Mass. The firm
voices of the bride and bridegroom echoed up around
the vast dome and were clearly heard by everyone
present.

When the party emerged into the July sunshine a
cheering crowd awaited them on the steps, and the
word 'Beautiful!' was heard in several different lan-
guages and accents.

'*Mio Dio*, we shall be mobbed!' muttered the
groom out of the side of his mouth. Even the passing

vaporetti slowed and sounded their horns in honour of the bride.

With Pino on one side of her and Count Favaro on the other, Lucia made her way down the steps, followed by Sir Peter, flanked on either side by Lady Philippa and the contessa. Gianni Scogliera must have felt that the bridesmaid also needed protection, for he stepped forward to take her arm firmly in his.

The barges set out on the return journey to the Lido with the guests on board but without the newly wedded couple: on an impulse Pino led his wife to a gondola moored at the quayside.

'Come with me in a gondola, *amore mio*—we have never sailed in one before!' he urged her, and the straw-hatted gondolier was delighted with the lovely passenger who settled herself into the cushioned chair beside her husband.

Tremendous applause rose from the bystanders, and a regular convoy of small craft followed them as they glided away across the mouth of the Grand Canal, past St Mark's and the Doge's Palace on the Riva degli Schiavoni and into the basin—or kiss— of St Mark's.

'This is the happiest day of my life, Lucia *mia*,' said Pino as he kissed his wife with an almost reverent tenderness.

'And I am the happiest woman in Venice, *caro* Pino,' she assured him, nestling in the haven of his encircling arm with her head on his shoulder.

The gondolier tactfully turned away, setting the prow southwards to the Lido—taking his passengers on their way to their reception and their new life together, across the sparkling waters of the Lagoon.

MILLS & BOON®

Medical Romance™

COMING NEXT MONTH

A GIFT FOR HEALING by Lilian Darcy
Camberton Hospital

Karen Graham's manipulative ex-boyfriend, who was sick with TB, wanted her back. Guilt-ridden, she had no-one to turn to except Lee Shadwell. He was more than willing to offer friendship and support. Karen knew she was loved and in love, but with which man?

POWERS OF PERSUASION by Laura MacDonald

Nadine vowed to remain immune to the charms of the new Italian registrar Dr Angelo Fabrielli. But that proved impossible when he moved into her house—and her heart! But she refused to be his wife knowing that she could never give him the one thing he needed most...

FAMILY TIES by Joanna Neil

The new locum, Dr Matthew Kingston, was critical and a touch too arrogant so Becky Laurens kept her distance. But that proved difficult when she found him incredibly attractive. Becky had to end things with her current boyfriend—but was Matthew willing to take his place?

WINGS OF CARE by Meredith Webber
Flying Doctors

Radio operator, Katy Woods, was secretly in love with Dr Peter Flint. So when he was trapped during a cyclone she willingly offered words of comfort. And on his return Peter made it clear that he wanted Katie! But did he want commitment?

Available from WH Smith, John Menzies, Volume One, Forbuoys, Martins, Woolworths, Tesco, Asda, Safeway and other paperback stockists.

MILLS & BOON®

TO HAVE & TO HOLD

Celebrate the joy, excitement and sometimes
mishaps that occur when planning that special
wedding in our treasured four-story collection.

Written by four talented authors—
Barbara Bretton, Rita Clay Estrada,
Sandra James and Debbie Macomber

Don't miss this wonderful short story collection
for incurable romantics everywhere!

Available: April 1997   Price: £4.99

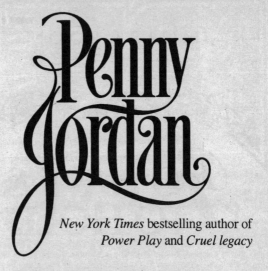

Penny Jordan

New York Times bestselling author of
Power Play and *Cruel legacy*

POWER GAMES

The arrival of a mysterious woman threatens
a son's manipulative hold over his
millionaire father in PENNY JORDAN'S
latest blockbuster—a supercharged tale of
family rivalries

**AVAILABLE IN PAPERBACK
FROM MARCH 1997**

FOUR FREE
specially selected
Medical Romance™ novels
<u>PLUS</u> a FREE Mystery Gift
when you return this page...

Return this coupon and we'll send you 4 Medical Romance novels and a mystery gift absolutely FREE! We'll even pay the postage and packing for you.

We're making you this offer to introduce you to the benefits of the Reader Service™– FREE home delivery of brand-new Medical Romance novels, at least a month before they are available in the shops, FREE gifts and a monthly Newsletter packed with information, competitions, author profiles and lots more...

Accepting these FREE books and gift places you under no obligation to buy, you may cancel at any time, even after receiving just your free shipment. Simply complete the coupon below and send it to:

MILLS & BOON READER SERVICE, FREEPOST, CROYDON, SURREY, CR9 3WZ.

READERS IN EIRE PLEASE SEND COUPON TO PO BOX 4546, DUBLIN 24

NO STAMP NEEDED

Yes, please send me 4 free Medical Romance novels and a mystery gift. I understand that unless you hear from me, I will receive 4 superb new titles every month for just £2.20* each, postage and packing free. I am under no obligation to purchase any books and I may cancel or suspend my subscription at any time and the free books and gift will be mine to keep in any case.
(I am over 18 years of age)

M7XE

Ms/Mrs/Miss/Mr _____
BLOCK CAPS PLEASE
Address_____

_____

_____ Postcode _____

MILLS & BOON®

Back by Popular Demand

BETTY NEELS

COLLECTOR'S EDITION

A collector's edition of favourite titles from one of the world's best-loved romance authors.

Mills & Boon are proud to bring back these sought after titles, now reissued in beautifully matching volumes and presented as one cherished collection.

Don't miss these unforgettable titles, coming next month:

Title #23 THE PROMISE OF HAPPINESS
Title #24 SISTER PETERS IN AMSTERDAM

Available wherever
Mills & Boon books are sold